SAVING HER RESCUER

A BILLIONAIRE & A VIRGIN ROMANCE

MICHELLE LOVE

HOT AND STEAMY ROMANCE

CONTENTS

About the Author   v
Sign Up to Receive Free Books   vii

Blurb   1
1. Chapter One   4
2. Chapter Two   10
3. Chapter Three   18
4. Chapter Four   28
5. Chapter Five   36
6. Chapter Six   42
7. Chapter Seven   52
8. Chapter Eight   57
9. Chapter Nine   65
10. Chapter Ten   71
11. Chapter Eleven   82
12. Chapter Twelve   86
13. Chapter Thirteen   91

    Sign Up to Receive Free Books   95
    Preview of Secrets & Desires   96
    Chapter One   98
    Chapter Two   107
    Chapter Three   118
    Chapter Four   127
    Chapter Five   131
    Chapter Six   140
    Chapter Seven   149

Other Books By This Author   163
About the Author   165
Copyright   167

Made in "The United States by:

Michelle Love

© Copyright 2020 – Michelle Love

ISBN: 978-1-64808-092-0

ALL RIGHTS RESERVED. No part of this publication may be reproduced or transmitted in any form whatsoever, electronic, or mechanical, including photocopying, recording, or by any informational storage or retrieval system without express written, dated and signed permission from the author

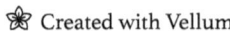 Created with Vellum

ABOUT THE AUTHOR

Mrs. Love writes about smart, sexy women and the hot alpha billionaires who love them. She has found her own happily ever after with her dream husband and adorable 6 and 2 year old kids.
Currently, Michelle is hard at work on the next book in the series, and trying to stay off the Internet.
"Thank you for supporting an indie author. Anything you can do, whether it be writing a review, or even simply telling a fellow reader that you enjoyed this. Thanks

Facebook
   facebook.com/HotAndSteamyRomance

SIGN UP TO RECEIVE FREE BOOKS

Sign Up to Receive Free E-Books and Audiobook Codes.

Would you like to read **The Unexpected Nanny, Dirty Little Virgin** and **other romance books** for **free**?

You can sign up to receive these free e-books and audiobooks by typing this link into your browser:

https://www.steamyromance.info/free-books-and-audiobooks-hot-and-steamy/

Or this one:

https://www.steamyromance.info/the-unexpected-nanny-free/

BLURB

An icy road causes a ten-car pileup in the Adirondacks. Boston native Bethany O'Dell, who just turned nineteen, is one of the victims. She gets rescued when local billionaire recluse Henry Frakes, also involved in the crash, breaks into her car to get her out. Half caught in a flashback of his lover's death in a similar crash that was partly his fault, he talks feverishly about "saving you this time", and carries her to safety before disappearing.

Fascinated, she runs a search on Henry, who is known for owning an enormous, castle-like stone villa in the mountains nearby. She discovers that he made his fortune mysteriously, was subject to an IRS investigation that was later dropped, and was in a terrible car accident twenty years ago that killed his lover.

Henry is a gentle man with a dark past, who lives off investments he made back when he was operating one of the largest, longest-lasting on-line fences of stolen goods in the world. He has been alone since distracted driving from arguing with his girlfriend over his business led their car into the path of a speeding drunk driver. The impact killed her instantly, and Henry went into shock. Already wealthy, he became fabulously so in the two decades after Cara's loss, but never dated or touched a woman again.

When curious young journalist Bethany chases him down and disturbs his solitude, she gets the whole story...and an enormous crush on him. Worried about how depressed he seems, she stays with him that night. Henry screams himself awake that night, and when she goes to comfort him they end up making love intensely. But remembering his almost trance state during her rescue, she wonders if he's making love to her, or thinks he's sleeping with Cara.

Uncertain but sexually hooked, she stays the weekend, soon learning that he's quite dominant in bed, and a bit outside of it. The two are falling for each other, but when she discovers that she looks almost exactly like his dead girlfriend, her doubts nearly tear the budding relationship apart.

Bethany:

I was just trying to get away from my crazy ex for the weekend when I ended up in a giant pileup on the highway up to Gore Mountain. I wasn't hurt, but I was trapped in my car. Then this guy shows up out of nowhere, frees me, carries me to safety ... then calls me by the wrong name and disappears before I can thank him. I've got to find out who this hot, mysterious older guy is. Who is Henry Frakes, and why did he call me Cara? And when things heat up between us, is it me he's seeing in his arms ... or her?

Henry:

She's the very image of the wife I lost twenty years ago on that same damned stretch of road. But Bethany's her own person, and I'm still dealing with the scars of that terrible day. When I got stuck in that pileup, I ended up in a flashback. But this time, I saved Cara. Until I came out of it and realized that I had rescued someone else. Maybe I have a type. Maybe Bethany is Cara reincarnated. I have demons to battle before I can claim Bethany as my own, but they're all inside my head ... mostly.

CHAPTER ONE

Bethany

I make my way up to Gore Mountain as soon as the roads are clear, thinking only of getting out of Boston. It's a chilly five-hour drive to the Adirondacks, but I don't care. That's five hours between me and my battered apartment with its boarded-over window and punch marks in one wall—and between me and Michael, who did the damage.

I knew we wouldn't last when he started flirting with my classmates, but I never expected him to melt down completely like this when I dumped him. *And after I caught him cheating in our own bed!*

The fading bruise under my eye still stings after three days. Michael committed two deal-breakers in the span of two hours that night. One of them got him a night in jail, and an emergency protection order against him.

He knows we're quits. But he refuses to let go. This morning I caught him waiting outside my door in the apartment hallway He even had the balls to be pissed that I changed the locks.

So, he's spending another few nights in jail, for violating the protection order. And I'm taking a badly-needed break from Boston.

I couldn't sleep comfortably in my apartment with so many reminders of Michael around. So I pulled out a chunk of my savings, made a hotel reservation, and took off for the Adirondacks.

I reach the highway and the traffic thins, and I breathe a sigh of relief. I hate driving in Boston. The motorists there practically *try* to hit each other.

But that's where school is, and home until I'm done with school. I was lucky to get my apartment—just like I'm lucky that my internship, scholarship money and the money from my blog add up to enough to pay for it. So I manage, for now.

My idea of a break always involves getting out of town for a while, and away from the press of people. This time, the feeling is just a bit more urgent than usual. *Thanks, Michael, you horse's ass.*

I've missed Gore Mountain for years. I haven't had the cash to visit much since I left home, but I have always dreamed of coming back. I used to ski myself sore there every winter: sore and sunburnt and numb-nosed from the icy wind whipping by.

There's no more peaceful feeling for me than racing down a mountain slope alone.

I'm hoping to recapture it this weekend, and cleanse my aching heart. That's the reason I'm risking going up there so soon after a round of unseasonably heavy snowstorms. At least the temperature's already rising above freezing.

I feel my spirits lift as I put some music on and prepare myself mentally for the long haul ahead. *Between the fresh snow on the slopes, the warmer spring weather and the thinner crowds, the resort should be lovely for unwinding.*

That damned idiot Michael will still be trying to call me once they let him out, but I can screen my calls. He constantly violates the protection order, no matter how often he gets reported and picked up for it. Yet another reason for me to get out of town for a while.

Go to Hell, Michael. If he keeps this garbage up, he can see how well his uselessness, whining and abusive bullshit goes over in General Population.

I start to really relax after about the first hour of driving. I stop poking at my bruise, some of the tension leaves my muscles, and I even catch myself humming along to AC/DC on the radio. By the time I stop for lunch at a tiny roadside diner three hours into my drive, I'm even smiling.

See? I tell myself as I pull into the parking lot. *You can do this. Life can go on. It didn't end when Michael lost his shit and started breaking things.*

The diner is a weird steak and burger place with rustic timber decor and a mobster theme. Movie posters line the walls: *The Godfather, King of New York, Prizzi's Honor*. A badly edited TV version of *Goodfellas* plays on the television.

A line-faced waitress with red-dyed hair and too much makeup smiles at me as she brings me a menu and some water. I sip it as I page through the offerings.

I almost order the diet plate on reflex: salad and an unappetizing-sounding ground turkey patty. But then I remember *Michael's gone* and smile, and order a bacon cheeseburger.

How many times did we eat out only for him to stare at me and make disapproving noises when I ate more than would sustain a kitten? Every damn time. He wanted me bony, but I don't skinny down that much without getting sick.

So now, I'm going to enjoy myself a little. Maybe I'll even have a milkshake. I'll be burning it off on the slopes soon enough.

Now that I have left Boston behind, it's like a weight has

lifted off of me. I got a little too used to the burden of Michael, I realize. Now that I'm free, I feel myself coming to life inside.

And suddenly I'm horny as hell.

Sex with Michael was about as satisfying as gas station pizza: unexciting, barely filling, without real nourishment, and sometimes a little bit sickening. As I look around the half-filled cafe at the truckers and tourists who have also stopped for a bite, my eyes trace over every unaccompanied man with the excited curiosity of the newly free.

Well. All except the young blond guy. Michael has killed my taste for that type, probably for good.

That's fine; the lodge will be full of athletic men, and some will be single. *I'm free of him. I can look around. Date. Get laid by someone who actually knows and cares about what he's doing.*

What an intriguing idea. Also a first for me, but I know men like that are actually out there. I've heard my girl friends raving about this or that wild weekend, and one or two are already planning their weddings. I've just had crappy luck, I guess.

That's okay. *My time will come. Maybe even this weekend.*

What I really want is a rare animal: a guy who actually treats me well *and* has skill and patience in bed. That probably means someone older than me, way more mature than boys my age, and more...experienced.

But will I be able to attract someone like that? The only problem with older guys is that so many of them seem to be looking for someone naive as well as young and hot. I haven't been naive in years; just too kind-hearted for my own good.

I follow my burger up with a mocha as I watch the room, then get back on the road once my meal settles. I'm headed up into the Adirondacks now, and the snow I left behind in Boston now starts to streak the sides of the road again as I gain elevation.

Soon enough, I reach the real snow country, up where the

plows are still working, and the wind blows clouds of shimmering white off the slopes above. The new snowfall has loaded down the evergreens that flank the road so thickly that their branches bend toward the ground. Sometimes, the quickly-melting burden slides off in chunks, and the dark green branches bound skyward, throwing the rest off in glittering arcs.

Now and again, my car passes a clear slope that gleams like a pearl in the strengthening sun. I can't wait to get my skis on when I see them. But we're still a ways from Gore Mountain yet, and I need to be patient, and focus on the road.

The traffic starts thickening as I get closer to the resort. I slow down, ignoring the honks from impatient people behind me. The snow has redeposited on the highway in places, making it slippery and treacherous.

Now and again, a fresh cloud of snow overtakes the road briefly, blown by the wind that screams down the slopes and sometimes makes my car rock. I cut on my fog lights and slow down further, wary of a spring avalanche. You don't fall in love with the snow without understanding all the ways that it can kill you.

The guy right behind me keeps laying on his horn, not seeming to notice how the blown snow from off the mountain keeps getting thicker around us. I pull to the side and let his battered SUV roar past, and he yells something obnoxious at me in a Jersey accent. *Yeah, yeah, asshole. Try not to drive off the cliff.*

Then something strange happens. The cloud of white in front of me suddenly becomes so dense that it seems to swallow the SUV entirely, along with every car near it. I frown, slowing further—and suddenly hear the scream of tires and feel the ground start to shake.

Oh fuck! I brake and pull over—but too late. The rumble becomes a roar—and suddenly the screech of tires turns into shattering glass and tearing metal.

I try to back up but there's nowhere to go. The cars behind me are starting to smash into each other. I feel someone run into my back bumper, pushing me forward into the snow cloud.

"No!" I yank the wheel futilely. Chunks of wet snow slam against my windshield; I let out a scream of shock and fear. Then something hits the side of my car so hard that it goes tumbling side-over-side into the air...and right off the cliff's edge.

I hear a hard thud, and the crunch of glass. The seatbelt digs into my shoulder, and I black out.

CHAPTER TWO

Bethany

I open my eyes to an upside-down world. My windows are completely white outside but are amazingly intact; the car's functional enough that I can see the glow of the headlights faintly through the layer of snow. I'm conscious, alive..and in a crazy situation.

I flip on the emergency lights, praying someone will see them in the blowing snow, then do a quick check-in with myself. My head hurts, one shoulder feels wrenched, and I'm sure I'll have bruises from the seatbelt I'm hanging from. But I'm not bleeding, I can feel my feet, and nothing seems broken.

Holy shit. I close my eyes, trying to focus past my fear. *That was an avalanche. I just got hit by a damn avalanche and survived!*

So far, anyway.

"Okay," I tell myself, my voice strangely loud in the small space. "Emergency lights are on and flashing. This is a major highway. Rescue crews are coming.

"Someone will notice me. I'll be able to get air, and I'll be able to stay warm until they dig me out." I have to stop and draw a sobbing breath as I weather another wave of fear. "I'm only partly buried, and it's still daylight."

It's okay. I'll be free soon. Someone will come.

The onslaught of logic-based reassurances works well enough that I stop shaking. I finally take another deep breath and open my eyes. My head is pounding from being upside down, but I don't seem to have hit it.

Another plus: I don't smell gasoline.

I still have to get out of here. The sudden understanding hits me hard, along with the realization that drives it: what if there's another avalanche before someone can reach me? I could be knocked off whatever my car's come to rest on and go tumbling into the ravine. Or I could simply end up buried beyond recovery.

Yeah, fuck staying. I brace myself against the roof and unlatch my seatbelt, huffing slightly as I fall from it and bang my knees against the steering wheel. The avalanche hit me broadside; the trees on the slope of the ravine must have broken my car's fall. Fortunately, wherever my car is wedged, it is at least temporarily stable.

I reposition myself awkwardly in the small space, setting my shoulder against the door and shoving as I work its latch. It moves barely an inch—but then stops, wedged shut by the weight of the frozen mess beyond. "Fuck!"

I turn around and put my feet against the door, bracing myself and shoving against it with all the strength in my legs. It barely moves another inch; snow falls onto my ankles, and a little fresh air trickles in, but that's it. I'm completely trapped.

Tears of pure terror blur my vision for a moment. I dash them away and set my jaw, repeating my reassurances. *No need to panic. Someone will get to me. I just have to get their attention.*

Fortunately, the horn is still working.

I honk it in intervals: ten seconds on, ten seconds off to

nervously listen. During those desperate in-between times, I can hear distant, muffled noises: sirens, walkie-talkies, occasional cries of dismay. *How many people were hit by the avalanche, or piled up their cars because they couldn't stop in time?*

How many people died?

That thought makes me sick. Tears of fear and despair fill my eyes again, but I keep working the horn. *Whatever happens, I'm not going to join them!*

The battery will run out eventually. I'm terrified of what could happen then—when the horn goes silent and the lights go dark. The heater will stop working then too.

But I don't dare run the engine to recharge the battery. With no idea what shape it's in, I could start a fire.

This is not how I plan to go out, damn it! My breath shivers; I'm trembling. But I still fight to keep focused. *I can still survive. Someone will save me.*

Someone...please save me.

The horn is starting to lose its strength and the lights flicker and dim when I suddenly hear the crunch of footsteps coming toward me. Just one pair, heavy and purposeful. "Hello?" I call out at the top of my lungs, and then honk the horn again.

The footsteps walk right up to the driver's side of the car, and after a moment, I hear the snow crunch in a different way, and shift. Then again. Someone is digging.

I hold my breath, not wanting to distract the stranger with any more yelling and honking. The steady crunch of the shovel biting away chunks of snow grows closer, and eventually I can hear the low, masculine grunts of effort behind it.

Oh thank God, it must be a rescue worker. I sag with relief; they have finally gotten to me. Or...someone else has.

The shovel clacks hard against my driver's side window, and I flinch away from it. Whoever is digging me out pauses, and I see a black-gloved hand brush the last layer of snow away from the window.

A face peers in at me: long and handsome, with piercing green eyes that have crows' feet at the corners. He stares in at me with a stunned expression for a few seconds...and then straightens and starts digging the rest of the snow away from the door. His movements are frantic now, and I wait breathlessly for him to finish.

Finally, he tosses aside the shovel and grabs a crowbar out of the snowbank. I watch him use it to scrape the snow and ice away from the crack in the door, then laboriously pry it open.

Finally it opens with a jerk and I bolt forward, practically crashing into his legs in my effort to get out of that car. He drops the crowbar and catches me, wrapping his arms around me to steady me.

"It's all right, Cara," he mumbles in a deep, strangely distracted voice. "I've got you. I saved you this time."

"Oh God, that was crazy. Thank you." Then what he said registers and I blink up at him, completely lost. "Sorry, what?"

He smiles dreamily, then easily scoops me up. He's a big man, fit, his body broad-shouldered and hard under his insulated clothes. "We'll have the paramedics check you out, and then we'll go home. You'll be okay."

I don't protest; I feel wobbly suddenly, my muscles shaking. I'm still lost on why he called me Cara...but as he carries me up the steep, snow-clogged slope and onto the road, I'm suddenly too distracted to care.

The avalanche completely blocks the highway. Cars, trucks and SUVs are caught in it, twisted and sometimes smoking. The one that passed me up earlier is halfway down the ravine, fetched up against a shattered stand of trees.

I stare at the twisted shape, crushed like a beer can in a

drunk's fist, and my eyes blur with tears. *Why the hell didn't you slow down?*

Even worse is the pile-up just before the avalanche. At least ten cars lie all over the icy road, sometimes in pieces. Six ambulances, a search and rescue team and a highway team with digging equipment are all hard at work dealing with the mess.

I gasp in horror, and the stranger's grip tightens on me. "Shh, sh. It's okay, try to stay calm. We just have to make sure you're not hurt."

I nod mutely, burying my face against his strong shoulder. Three tow trucks pull away as he climbs over the mound of snow and crushed cars with me in his arms. I stare at the chewed-up messes the trucks are dragging and realize that I was incredibly lucky. Their occupants are probably dead.

I could be too, right now. But instead, I have my hero out of nowhere, with his gentle hands and hazy eyes. He keeps doggedly carrying me toward the small army of ambulances at the far end of the mess.

He smells really nice: woodsmoke, leather, bay rum aftershave. His breath smells like mint gum and coffee, and he cradles me against him like I'm something precious.

"What's your name?" I ask him, intrigued.

"You know my name, sweetheart," he murmurs with that distracted smile. I suddenly realize that he's in some kind of shock as well.

Oh shit. What's going on with this guy? "Are you okay?"

"I am now that I know you're safe. But I can't say the same for the Lexus." His voice is low and thoughtful, very serious—but his eyes stay hazed over, and I start to wonder if he's hit his head. At least his pupils are the same size.

"Maybe you should have the paramedics look at you too," I suggest very tentatively.

My hair blows into my eyes and he brushes it out of them

almost tenderly. I'm confused, liking the sensation but too overwhelmed to think about it much.

He plods on tirelessly. "I'll be fine. I don't have a scratch on me. Let's just get you checked out."

I keep quiet until he carries me easily over to an unoccupied ambulance. "Hey," he calls out. "I just peeled my lady here out of that upside-down Dodge. She was the one on the horn. Anyone free?"

He seems completely lucid now, and I'm...not, I realize. My legs and arms are shaking, and though my heart has slowed down, my whole body feels weak from all the adrenaline that has run through me.

The exhausted-looking crew members look up: two men and a woman, each nursing a coffee. One of the men downs his and sets his thermos aside to come help my rescuer bundle me into the back of the ambulance.

"How long were you trapped?" the shaven-headed guy asks as he takes my blood pressure.

"I don't know. It can't have been too long, my car still had power for a while." I squint as he shines a pen light in my eyes. "I was unconscious for a bit, but I think that was the shock."

"Any pain? Did you hit your head?"

"Not that I can remember." I answer his list of questions on autopilot as I look over at the man who saved me. He's watching me carefully, but has moved back, letting the medics do their work.

Who is he? He seems reluctant to give his name...but he also looks strangely familiar. Not very many guys are that memorable-looking. But where have I seen him before?

Miraculously, I still have my phone. I forgot it in all the chaos. I pull it out and snap a few photos of the guy.

Seeing me do that, he playfully pulls out his phone and does the same to me. The way he smiles...his tender manner. *Has he mistaken me for someone else?*

That has to be it. It's the only thing besides my totally misreading the situation that makes any sense. He's just a big, brave, charming flirt who's trying to keep me from falling into a panic or depression after rescuing me.

He could also be delusional in some way. But the way that his heroics, his kindness, his scent and his touch have all caught my attention make me *really* hope it's not that.

"Okay, you've suffered a bad shock, and some bruising, especially across your shoulder. The good news is, it's nothing ibuprofen, fluids and sleep won't fix. We're waiting for a transport bus to take everyone to town. Were you headed for the ski resort?" The paramedic hands me a cup of cocoa.

"Yeah," I murmur, still keeping an eye on the man who saved me. He's lowering his phone, and looks confused. "I have a reservation at the Gore Mountain Lodge."

When I look up again, Mystery Guy's on the phone talking to someone.

"You'll have to rent a car in town and move your stuff there tomorrow. For tonight we're putting everyone up at a local motel while the injured go to the hospital. Was there anyone with you besides your husband?"

I look up at the paramedic suddenly, feeling my cheeks burn. "Oh, uh, he's not my husband. He just saved me. Came out of nowhere, actually."

"Huh." He frowns over at the man, who seems to be arguing with someone. Then he grabs a clipboard and hands it to me. "Okay, well, here you go.

"Just put down your contact information and the details about your car. We're gonna haul it off for you. We'll drop it at the mechanic's if it can't be driven. Otherwise we'll bring it to the motel parking lot."

"Thank you," I manage, feeling a slow trickle of relief. This is crazy, and scary, and disruptive, but it is only a setback. I will be all right. I can drive up to the resort and go skiing tomorrow, if I'm not too sore.

I look up to thank my rescuer as well—and blink in shock, looking around. He's gone...just as suddenly as he arrived.

CHAPTER THREE

Henry

"It was Cara. I swear to God that it was, Uncle Jake."

Jake's been making us dinner while he listens to the news on his phone. The avalanche and the crash are all over it right now. He looks up from rough-chopping a length of pepperoni, his expression pained.

"Henry...Cara's dead. You know that."

I take a deep breath. He said the same thing to me on the phone, while I was looking right at her. Cara, my love, my wife, whom I buried almost twenty years ago.

I saved you this time, I think, licking my dry, chilled lips as a sense of unreality washes over me. *I finally managed it.*

Logically, I know that my uncle's right. His hard, worried look drags my feet back onto the ground: flight of fancy over.

Not my wife at all. Too young, and way too...alive. But how the Hell do you explain this?

"I know," I say, holding my hands up. "You're right. Cara's been dead for two decades now, and I know that.

"But this woman literally looked just like her. Same hair, same eyes, same build—"

"You had a flashback, Henry," he says with just the slightest edge of frustration to his voice. "You rescued some woman because you thought she was Cara. But she wasn't. Now please, tell me you really know that."

I sigh in exasperation, and pull out my phone. I unlock it, pull up the photos I took of her, and hand it over to him. "Here. See for yourself."

He sets down his knife, then slowly takes the phone. His eyes widen as he stares down at the first photo. "Holy shit."

He looks up at me, blinking slowly, then looks back down at the phone screen again. "...Okay. I get it, I'm lots less worried about your mental state now—but that is genuinely fucking weird."

"The woman I rescued *does* look exactly like my Cara." *I'm not crazy—or at least, not quite that crazy.*

"So much so that I'm wondering if Cara had a cousin. But this girl's too young. Did you get her name?" He's still staring at me piercingly, as if still not quite trusting my grip on reality.

I can't blame him, even if I resent his doubts sometimes. Losing Cara broke me, and he's the one who has been helping me put the pieces back together. But today, my progress got seriously challenged.

That crash threw me into the most profound flashback I have had in six years. Suddenly, I was back in my truck with Cara, everything shattered around us: Cara unconscious and bleeding from the head. But a moment later, I was alone in my smashed Lexus surrounded by deployed airbags, and she was gone.

So I went looking for her. And I found that girl instead. "Yeah, I was flashing back, but can you blame me? She was real, and she really looked like...that."

Like my Cara. Lovely Cara, my wife of eighteen months, whom I married just out of high school. It makes me ache just thinking about it.

We were both dizzily in love, and had no idea that forces had already been set in motion to rip her from my arms for good. No idea that it would be my own mistakes that would force me to stumble on without her, heart and mind in pieces. But that is exactly what happened, and ever since then, I've lived with the guilt.

Today, though, I almost feel like I started working off my crime. It doesn't bring Cara back, but an innocent girl with her face is now alive thanks to me.

I've really got Uncle Jake's attention now. He seems a lot less worried...but a lot more confused. "That's one hell of a mind-fuck. Did you get her name?"

I shake my head, regretting it. "No. I was too disoriented...especially once you and I started arguing over the phone. Not that I'm blaming you. I wish I had gotten her name and phone number."

He lets out a low grunt, looking thoughtful, then peers at me. "What happened to the Lexus? You hurt?" He hands me back my phone and goes back to chopping.

"Totaled. But the safety measures did their job. I could use a trip to my chiropractor, but that's it."

"That was lucky. What shape is the girl's car in?" He finishes with the pepperoni and starts chopping mushrooms and a few kinds of olives together.

I sit down at the kitchen table, mouth watering. I know better than to get in his way when he's cooking. He's territorial in the kitchen. "Upside down in a snowbank ten feet down the slope. Good thing she was wearing her seatbelt at the time."

Unlike Cara. God, Cara... I shake it off, and look down at the tired, bruised girl on my phone. Not Cara, but real, and her spitting image. And safe now, because of me.

Shocked, flashing back, and I still managed to save someone's life. That's not bad at all.

My uncle chops away, keeping half an eye on me. "Sounds like the poor kid had a really shitty day. But it probably would have been worse if you weren't there."

"I was just thinking that." *Bruised.* I peer distractedly at the image. "That's strange."

"Eh? What's that?" He pauses in his work again and looks my way.

"The bruise under her eye is developed. Maybe a few days old." The sleuth in me, lover of true crime novels and whodunit movies, focuses in on the detail. "...That's a shiner."

Someone hit her.

The sudden, intense surge of rage takes me completely by surprise. I know in the back of my head that it's because she looks like Cara. The idea of someone slamming his fist into that face makes me want to find him, and beat him until he can't move.

"Henry." My uncle's voice is sharp.

"It looks like she was attacked." *I should do something. If not to him, then for her.*

"Leave it, Henry."

I look up at him, a mix of puzzled and annoyed. "What?"

He sighs through his nose. "Leave it. She is a complete stranger, and it is her business. Let me make the goddamn calzones, let's have supper, and let's watch *The Maltese Falcon* like normal people.

"I know she looks like Cara. I know you miss that girl so much that you haven't touched another woman since. I know you punish yourself all the damn time, too."

He took a deep breath, and stared at me pointedly. "If having helped this girl makes you hate yourself a little less, then good for you. But don't go chasing her."

That shouldn't piss me off, but it does. She can't have been put in my path for no reason. It's too much of a coincidence that a girl the very image of my dead wife should end up in a car accident on the same stretch of road, only to be rescued by me.

Do I believe in reincarnation? I have never even considered it before today. But even if that crazy theory is somehow right, do I have any right to chase after some new incarnation of Cara, after failing her so badly last time?

Whoever this girl is, if I come at her with all of this, she would probably think I'm completely crazy. I might even scare her away completely. And what would it accomplish?

I may not even have the right to pursue her. My task may simply have been to save her this time, and be satisfied that she is alive and happy in the world somewhere.

But then the image of the bruise on her cheek rises in my mind, and my fists clench on the tabletop. *Is she happy, though? Is she safe?*

"You're not saying anything," my uncle observes as he finishes chopping olives.

"I'm just wondering if she's doing okay."

The knife thwacks against the chopping block a little too hard. "Henry. For the last time, this is not good for you. You want to end up with a restraining order against you for scaring some stranger because you miss your wife? This self-punishing shit has to stop."

He's right. I know it in my gut. I will probably alarm the girl if I go tracking her down.

Fuck. My heart sinks as I think about it, but I finally sigh and nod. "You're right. I won't pursue her. But I sure am curious why she looks so much like Cara."

I see his shoulders sag with relief, and he goes right back to kitchen prep. "Good. So am I, but you know how you get."

"Yeah." *But what about the bruise?* "I know how I get."

That evening, having missed my afternoon workout, I make up for it brutally, filling my home gym with a hard-rock soundtrack and the clangs, thumps and pulley-creaks of exercise equipment. I've been obsessed with fitness since junior high, when I learned how a well-toned body and some practice could protect both myself and Cara from the neighborhood bullies.

We met and made friends in seventh grade after I moved in with my uncle. Back then, our family was poor, and his veteran's pension allowed him a small house in Poughkeepsie, and nothing more. She lived just down the road, and walked past my house every morning on her way to school.

I realized that she was being bullied when she asked me to walk with her. I was shy, but one look at the fear in those velvety eyes and I had to help her. Two years later she gave me my first kiss, and after that, I belonged to her.

I learned to fight, and worked out daily, with an extra run at night. I ate so much boiled chicken, eggs and yogurt those days that I started getting stomach aches. I wanted to make myself huge, a bulwark between Cara and the world.

Today, I run ten miles a day, or bike twenty. I have an hour of weight training, and an hour of judo practice. My routine back then was even more brutal.

I chuckle a little as I do crunches on my slant board, remembering. My abdominals gleam with sweat as they bunch and flex. These days, I'm pretty satisfied with my looks, speed and strength.

Back then, I was constantly frustrated, because I was building on a base of junior high reediness. Being an impressionable teen, I was also basing my expectations on the bodies I saw in comics and film—with teen boys drawn as or played by twenty-something men. So I was never satisfied with what I saw in the mirror.

But Cara was. The night she surprised me with that kiss, my heart walked off after her like a puppy. We were fifteen.

I started working out harder, joining the weight training class, track, martial arts courses. I wanted to look good for her. I wanted her to want to touch me.

We were sixteen when her scumbag father caught me walking her back from school. He demanded to know what I was doing and I explained about the big guys who kept lifting up her skirt at the bus stop. He somehow convinced himself I was gay because I didn't participate, and only because of that, trusted me with his daughter.

A year later, Cara slipped in my bedroom window after climbing up the rose trellis. For the first time, we could touch each other as much as we wanted. Giddy with excitement, trying to keep our voices down, we struggled to strip each other down under the covers. And then...

I groan through my teeth as I work through the last of my set. My memories have left my cock hard and throbbing, tenting my indigo workout shorts. I miss her even more now, and wonder again about the girl with her face.

Thoughts of her haunt me through my workout. I wonder if she would enjoy the same things in bed that Cara did. *That's a dangerous train of thought,* I warn myself, and try to focus on my workout.

A sauna and a cool shower leave me relaxed and sleepy enough for a novel and bed. I'm working my way through *Never Cry Wolf*. It's a much better read than expected, even compared to the movie, which is one of my favorites.

But as I struggle to enjoy it, my mind keeps going back to Cara's twin, with the haunted eyes and bruised face. My thoughts linger on her until I fall asleep.

We've been kissing for hours, our hearts beating wildly against each other as I revel in the feel of her soft, naked breasts against my chest. How did she know Uncle Jake would leave for his flight at ten, and would be gone for the whole weekend?

She came here. She took the risk. She came to me, and she brought condoms.

I can't believe my luck as I run my hands over her warm, soft curves, helping her wiggle out of her clothes. Her eyes stare up at me in the moonlight, bright with desire and trust. "I want you to do it," she whispers as she unties the drawstring of my sleep shorts. "I want you to do everything."

I almost blast my first load right into the fabric at her invitation, but manage to control my eagerness. Still, I'm overwhelmed—with her, with my gorgeous, brave girlfriend, who snuck in like a thief to bring me the night of my dreams.

I tremble on top of her, one thigh wedged between her legs and my hand running over the gorgeous, springy globe of her breast. I run my thumb over the nipple and she gasps aloud.

"Mm, feels good..." she whimpers, and I start stroking that tiny, silky nub of flesh, watching it tighten as she throws her head back and pants.

It's amazing. I sit up on my knees over her and start fingering both of them. She squirms, arching her back, her eyes wide with amazement. "Oh!" she cries, and I muffle her with my mouth as she whimpers and squeals.

My erection's so hard now that it hurts. I feel it throbbing against my belly through the fabric. Now and again, her squirming body brushes up against it, and I grunt into her mouth as I feel a tingle shoot through my body.

I break the kiss and move downward as she keeps writhing, enjoying the sounds of her trying to muffle her own gasps and moans behind her lips. Her body bucks under mine, offering the glorious softness of her breasts as I hover over them hungrily. Finally, unable to stand it, I start kissing her nipple, running my hand down her body instead.

Her body stiffens; she presses her breast against my mouth and I pounce on it, suckling eagerly. The taste of her skin, her softness, her trilling croons as she grabs double handfuls of my hair and starts to buck her hips, they all intoxicate me.

I slide an arm under her, propping myself on my elbow as I suckle her breast and feel her tremble and thrash under me. Her voice has gone to wordless, musical cries; she finally drags over a pillow and buries her face in it. I suck harder and hear her muffled squeal.

My hand finally works between us, pulling her panties down and shoving my shorts down to free my cock. She lifts her hips to help me, her thighs parting as she kicks free of the thin cotton...and then settling around me.

Everything in me aches to thrust into her, but somehow, I remember the condom. Rolling it on seems to take a million years as she pants and moans under me. My mouth works over her nipple, and then shifts and fastens onto the other just as I finish rolling the rubber over my pounding shaft.

My free hand drifts to her soft, sparsely-haired pussy, now slick with her juices, and I part her gently with my fingers. She pumps her hips harder as I stroke her. I look up, and see her head stretched back, every muscle taut as I suckle and caress.

Her body trembles, so tense that she practically lifts me off the bed. Her warm pussy bucks invitingly against my hand. Finally, unable to stand it, I fit the sheathed head of my cock into her warm opening and thrust into her.

Her nails rake my shoulders; she lets out a long moan—and my hand and mouth move on autopilot as her body takes my cock into its warm, slick embrace. I groan hoarsely against her breast, and then start thrusting in time with my caresses.

It's so good. Her body embraces me again and again as I sink into her, my hips pumping slowly...then faster and faster. Her legs tighten *around me; I can barely remember to keep fingering her, but I manage somehow.*

Her flesh starts to clench around me as her cries reach their peak; she goes up on her heels—and then grinds and shudders around me violently as I lose control and pound into her hard. I hear her voice from far away, calling out with joy—and then I soar up to join her.

I wake covered in hot sweat and groan, feeling my cock pumping out its load so hard it almost hurts. "*Cara—*" I gasp before I can stop myself. My hips thrust upward hard—and then I collapse to the mattress, shaking and tingling.

Oh, Baby, oh sweetheart...I miss you so fucking much.

It's been twenty years since I touched a woman. My sex drive hasn't exactly gone dormant...but I haven't had a dream like that in years. As I drag myself up and shower off, I wonder again: *who is she, this woman with my wife's face?*

CHAPTER FOUR

Bethany

"So you never even found out his name?" My therapist, Dr. Kaplan, leans forward, wearing an intrigued expression. Her West London accent gives a slight lilt to her words. She's a small Indian woman with bright black eyes that are often full of merriment.

"He disappeared before I could get a straight answer out of him. I asked the guy, but he acted like I should already know. But I swear, I would have remembered a hunk like that if I had met him before." I can't keep my voice from sounding wistful.

I dreamed about him all weekend; it was the most fun I had, since the wreck kind of messed everything else up. I ended up spending most of the weekend overseeing my car's repairs, and paying for them with the money I had meant to spend on food and ski passes.

I drove home still wondering who my rescuer was. Now, healing up from bruises this bright Boston Monday, I still can't get him out of my mind.

"The truth is that he seemed to be in some kind of...trance. I can't even describe it. He even called me by another name."

"Wait. He went to all that trouble to save your life because he thought you were someone else? That must have been a little disappointing." Her eyes twinkle teasingly, and I roll my eyes.

"Maybe, but I wasn't about to look a gift rescue in the mouth, if you know what I'm saying." I smile wryly...but then grow serious. "I really want to find him, Doctor. I want to at least say thanks. And if he turns out to be single..."

"Oho." Her eyebrows rise. "It's a little soon to be playing the field after that mess with Michael, don't you think?"

I blush down to my toes. She's right...but she's not right. "Michael can go fuck himself. I want to move on.

"The truth is, we've been broken up emotionally for months. The guy just wouldn't leave my damn apartment." My lips twist. "And then he stank up our bed with that club whore."

"Okay, fair enough, and I can see the appeal of chasing a better experience with a man." The corner of her mouth curls slightly. She's been happily married for almost longer than I've been alive; I wish I knew her secret. "But why this mystery man in particular?"

"Well it's not just gratitude. And it's not just because he's hot. Though he is really, *really* hot." I hear a giggle spill out of me and we both blink in surprise.

"Wow. You sound flustered for once in your life. He's *that* hot?"

"Oh yeah." I sigh, remembering. "Huge, soulful eyes...he picked me up like I was nothing. He even smelled good."

She laughs softly. "You know, you came back here with a story of being in a horrible car accident that ruined your vacation. But all you seem to be able to talk about is this man."

That brings me up short. *Wow, she's right.* "I...well...the crash was really scary. And I hated having my weekend ruined, especially after that shit that Michael pulled. But..."

She folds her hands in her lap as she faces me. "Take your time."

"When I thought I was going to die, that man was there for me. When I was waiting for my car to be fixed and delivered back to me, thinking about him helped me get through it. When I had to take painkillers just to get to sleep, I dreamed about him.

"Just meeting him made the situation better, and not just because he rescued me."

"That's kind of amazing." She looks down at the phone in my hands. "You said you had pictures?"

"I do. Here." I unlock my phone, open its gallery and hand it over, and watch her eyes widen slightly.

She sits back, flicking back and forth through the three photos I took. "Oh wow. He's a bit old for you, but still. Yum. And no wedding ring that I'm seeing."

My cheeks heat up again. "I um, noticed that."

She considers the photos, then nods and hands back the phone. Looking me in the eye, she says, "I think you should try to find out who he is."

That takes me completely by surprise. "Wait, really?"

She nods. "Definitely. I have not seen you so lively and happy since before you met Michael. I say, find out who he is, and if he is local to Gore Mountain, invite him to meet you at the lodge next weekend."

Next weekend. The bill to replace my car window and front bumper took a big bite out of my savings, and vacationing again will take another. But as she looks at me knowingly, I really consider it.

I just met the most captivating man I have ever encountered. He saved my life. All I have to find him is his picture—but maybe that's enough. I'm an investigative reporter, after all, even if I'm new at it. It's my job to track down the truth.

"I'll let you know what I decide," I say, hedging my answer in case something comes up. But I already know what I want to do.

The maintenance guy has come and gone by the time I get home, replacing the shattered window and damaged drywall. The manager has left me a scrawled note asking me to bring by a copy of the new key. I put it on my to-do list for tomorrow and turn on the lights as I walk inside.

My apartment is tiny but pretty, all hardwood, with a living room/kitchen combo, a closet-sized green-and-blue tiled bathroom, and a cubby of a bedroom. My office takes up the living room now that Michael is gone. The first thing I did once he went to jail was have the cheap sofa he spent most of his life on trashed and his belongings sent to his mother.

The apartment is finally warm again with the window replaced. I stretch, feeling my healing bruises ache a little, then grab a garbage bag and start hunting around the house for any further evidence of Michael's presence. The whole time, I think about my mystery man.

I bag up the cheap canned stew Michael liked so much, and throw out a pair of his boxers that I find under my bed. I clean his hairs from the drain, and vacuum every trace of him out of the area rug. I make sure he's off of my movie rental accounts, and that my WiFi password is changed.

The whole time, I'm not thinking of Michael. I'm done with him. The last of his shouts stopped echoing in my space over a week ago. He doesn't deserve another moment of my time.

I'm thinking instead of the man who saved my life, who called me Cara and cradled me tenderly with hands that could wrench a jammed car door open in one go. I'm wondering what his kiss would taste like, and what his body would feel like against mine, without the barrier of all those clothes.

I clean Michael's leftovers out of the fridge, and finish scrubbing the place down. Then I burn Nag Champa incense to clear the air. My mood lifts as the sweet, spicy smell fills my home.

As I sip my evening tea, I'm wondering what my mystery man is like in bed. Probably very gentle and tender...to start. But after that? *What's that big, strong hottie like when he loses control?*

I really want to find out.

I send the images of my rescuer from my phone to my laptop and start running image searches. I settle in with my tea and a bowl of raspberries, determined to stick out the search as long as it takes.

...And then I find him in the first five minutes.

Meet Henry Frakes, Upstate New York's Reclusive Billionaire

Henry Frakes isn't a very sociable man. It's nothing about other people, he reassures me quietly as we drink coffee in his spectacular nine-bedroom house in the Adirondacks. He simply likes his privacy.

A recent addition to the ranks of New York's wealthiest men, Frakes is not your average billionaire. Aside from his home, he lives quietly, hiking and fishing on his lands and occasionally traveling abroad. He is unmarried since losing his first wife in 1998 in an automobile accident near their home.

Frakes's passion, aside from his various charitable activities, is his home, which was featured last year in *House Beautiful*. The restored Gilded Age hunting lodge became a personal project for himself and his uncle fifteen years ago, and he has never stopped improving on it.

"I spend more time fixing it up myself these days instead of hiring guys. I did the paneling and shelves in the library, and made my office desk out of part of a ring of oak stumps.

The outer three edges were left raw and sealed. I'm pretty proud of how it turned out."

My eyes widen, lingering on the single photo. He's caught in mid-gesture as he speaks to the reporter, his eyes distracted-looking, just as they were with me.

That big, brave, humble man is a billionaire. In fact, he owns what my Aunt called "The Castle", a huge structure overlooking the highway on the way up to Gore Mountain. It's only a few miles from the avalanche site.

Were you going home when the avalanche hit? Was it the same stretch of road where you lost your wife? What kind of mental state did that leave you in?

Who are you, Henry, besides a rich widower who saves the lives of strangers?

I already know, though: He's my hero. Even if he went to so much trouble for someone he thought he knew, he didn't know who was in my car at all until he pried the door open.

He didn't have to know me to know I deserved to be helped. And that's yet another reason why I have to get to know him better.

"Damn it," I muttered. "Why can't the world have more guys like Henry in it, and less like that twat Michael?"

If he lives at the Castle, and is a recluse, then he'll very likely be home if I come visit. I've got some doubts: what if he's seeing someone? What if he gets angry that I violated his privacy?

I'm suddenly exhausted, thinking about it all. I've already walked a few miles and done my yoga, but my energy level's at a low ebb. *Probably because I'm still healing. Crap.*

I'm refilling my mug of tea when I hear my phone go off. I frown and turn, pulling it out. Unknown number.

I hesitate. It could be the police asking for a statement about my part in the accident. It could be my insurance. Or, it could be Michael.

I take a chance as I sit down in my computer chair. "This is Bethany O'Shea."

"Oh hey Babe! You finally picked up!" Michael's cheerful voice stings my ear and I flinch away from the phone, scowling at it like I half expect him to come crawling out of the screen.

"You're violating the no-contact order again, Michael. You know I don't want to hear from you." *Prick.* At least he isn't pulling this shit in person. But I'm still so pissed off about it that I almost hang up right that moment.

"Fuck the no-contact order, Babe, I know you're just playing hard to get." His fake cheerfulness deepens, and all I can think of for a panicky moment is calling the cops again before he shows up. But instead, I stay focused.

"No. You cheated on me, verbally abused me, threw a fit when I threw you out, broke my window, damaged my wall and then blackened my eye.

"I never want to hear from you again. I never want to see you again. Why are you too fucking stupid to get that?" My voice cracks with anger. I don't care.

He's shocked into silence for a few moments, and I feel the faintest hope that he'll just hang up. But then, infuriatingly, he laughs. "Okay, okay, I get it. You're still pissed at me. You need some time to cool off, pretend you're tough. I understand."

He will never understand. I let out a deep sigh. "You killed any chance of us reconciling when you hit me. That is why you're up on assault and battery charges, why you're banned from the building, why I changed my locks, and why I got the protection order."

"It's your fault all that happened! You weren't giving me your ass so I found someone who did! Then you got all bitchy about it so you got put in your place!" His voice goes louder and faster, until he's rapid-fire screaming into the phone.

It terrifies me for all of two seconds, and then I grit my teeth. *Just a tantrum from an adult baby.*

"Goodbye, Michael. I'm calling the police about your harassment. You're going to prison." I'm shaking with a mix of anger and adrenaline from being screamed at...but a wave of satisfaction washes over me as his enraged scream becomes a horrified one.

"Nooo!" And I cut him off with a tap on my screen.

"Ugh." I sit back in my chair, rolling my eyes. I need a nap.

But first, I have three phone calls to make: to the police department, to my therapist, and to the Lodge, to see if I can turn my refund into a reschedule.

I'm going back to Gore Mountain, and I'm going to thank Henry Frakes properly for saving my life. Given half a chance, I'll screw his brains out, too.

And Michael can just go bang on the door of my empty apartment all next weekend, until the landlord has him arrested again.

CHAPTER FIVE

Henry

I don't know how I manage to keep from looking for the young mystery woman whose life I saved, but I do. I know my uncle is right about my need to avoid obsessing over this. He's generally right about everything—especially my health.

Uncle Jack is the only person in the world who gives a damn about me any more. I know that part of the reason is that I dragged us both up out of poverty, and he figures he owes me. But I'm also the last remnant of his kid brother that exists in the world.

And finally, he simply cares. He's that kind of guy. That is why he took me in after Mom and Dad vanished on that cruise back when I was seven, and it's why he puts up with me today.

It's also why he warned me off of chasing a college girl who doesn't know me from Adam.

There's part of me that worries that I already made a bad impression by rescuing her in a semi-fugue state, and calling her by the wrong name. But at least I got her out safely. I figure that probably got me at least some of the benefit of the doubt.

Then I remind myself that it doesn't matter, because I will never see her again.

But I still wonder about her. And I still worry about the bruise around her eye, just faded enough to show the knuckle marks. But I'll never have the chance to ask who put his hands on her, so I need to stop thinking about it.

Instead, I'm back in my wood shop again. Ever since I got out of the Dark Web resale game, I've been mostly focused on fixing up and expanding on the aged buildings on my property. There's the hunting lodge, my uncle's cottage, the boathouse on the small roadside lake that descends from a waterfall basin, and the covered bridge to the road at the far end.

Today, I'm repairing an old rowboat amid the stink of sanded wood and spar varnish. The fume extractor just isn't quite doing the job today, and after a while, I go outside to take a breather.

The cold slaps me awake at once. Fat, wet spring snowflakes are falling through the willow branches. The ground has thawed enough that the snowflakes just vanish when they strike the rotting leaves.

I huff a sigh of relief at the smell of clean air, and look around at my land with a soft, sad smile. I still find myself wishing sometimes that I had someone to share all this with besides my aging uncle. A woman, lively and kind, who would come to my arms and my bed as eagerly as Cara once had.

But then the thought of Cara makes the guilt come back. I squeeze my eyes shut and lean back against a tree trunk, shaking my head. *I don't deserve anyone anyway, not after what I did.* Or failed to do. Same difference.

The sound of a car motor approaching catches my attention. My lands are on a private road, and we're not expecting guests.

Mail maybe, or a delivery? Curious, I pull off my dust mask and walk out across the lawn to the bluff that overlooks the road.

I look down—and am startled to see a slightly battered royal blue Dodge that looks very familiar driving up the road. My eyes widen, and I back away from the railing, blinking several times. *What in the Hell? It can't be!*

I look again. It is.

I don't know how the woman with Cara's face found me. But my stupid, rebellious heart soars with delight at once.

My uncle has retreated to his cottage; I can hear the sound of his power drill as he works on more cold frames. *Good,* I think, as I have no real desire to explain this to him just yet. I hurry over to the house to get cleaned up.

I feel like a kid meeting his date for prom, checking myself in the damn mirror more than once and tucking in my shirt hastily. As I hear her footsteps click along toward the door on the bluestone path outside, my heart starts pounding.

Her knock makes me jump even though I'm standing five feet away and expect it. *Christ. Chill out, Henry.*

I wait a breathless half-minute before opening the door to greet her.

She's standing there smiling, her body language a little nervous, limbs pulled together. She's in an orchid purple sweater and black puffer vest, and a fuzzy knit cap that matches the sweater sits on her shining hair like a crown. And best of all, the bruise has faded from her face.

"Hi!" she says. "I'm Bethany. You kind of saved my life last week, and I wanted to say thank you."

I blink down at her, unsure of what to say in response. I know I'm not dreaming, but that doesn't help my sense of disorientation. "Uh...yeah. I mean, I recognize you. Please, come in."

I step back to let her in, and she moves forward a little,

looking around with slowly widening eyes. My smile gets a little less awkward; I love my home, and even if I don't spend much time around people in general, I still love showing it off.

The soaring entryway has its own fireplace, and is tiled around the edges in green marble, with wood parquet in the middle. The walls are all carved wood, with curio shelves full of fossils, and paintings of wildlife, some of which were done by my mother.

"Your place is amazing," she says quietly. She turns that smile back on me, and it's like the sun warming my skin.

Bethany, I think, feeling an odd little spurt of joy at knowing her name. "How did you find me?"

"I'm a journalism intern. I used my investigation skills. That and your house is famous. I grew up nearby, so I knew about the Castle. Just didn't know the owner by sight."

Her smile turns apologetic as we stand by the fireplace warming up. "I'm sorry if I was a little bit of a mess when we last met. Shitty circumstances."

I chuckle and stretch my fingers toward the fire. *I was in full flashback mode and she's apologizing for her behavior?* "That's true. And that's okay. I wasn't in a normal state of mind either."

Her brows draw together, tone going concerned. "Yeah, I noticed. Were you all right?"

"Well, no, my car was totaled and blew every safety system saving my life. I had to kick a window out to escape. I wasn't really injured, but it was still a shock."

She blinks slowly. "Holy shit. I can imagine. You seemed pretty dazed.

"Of course, that means I should be even more grateful that you helped me out. You were going through your own problems." She sounds really impressed, evoking a swell of satisfaction inside of me.

"It...wasn't the first time I've survived a serious car crash. I had to do something for the others. For you." I hesitate. I don't know how much to tell her.

I gesture down the hall toward the kitchen. "Have you, uh, eaten yet?"

She smiles and shakes her head.

I warm up a couple of the leftover calzones in the toaster oven while I try to figure out what to say. Finally, I realize that although I'll have to avoid telling too much at once, I absolutely need to let her know the truth.

I can't lie to Cara's face—and up close, Bethany still looks like Cara. Only her scent is different; she likes spicy, musky, rich fragrances, while Cara had liked florals.

I can't tell if it's the sameness or the difference that turns me on more.

"I have a medical condition as a result of the first accident," I say slowly. "If you read the articles on my house you're probably aware of the crash that killed my wife."

She nods, her eyes full of soft sympathy. Not pity; she watches me intently, seeming to hang on my every word. "I did read about it. I wasn't going to bring it up."

"Well, the pile-up from the avalanche kind of brought it up," I say wryly. "That was the reason for my...state of mind."

"Oh. Well, I'm sorry about that. But again, I'm glad for your help. I might not be here now without it."

The confused look returns as she looks up at me. "Was that why you thought I was someone else at first?"

I blink, my heart sinking. *Definitely a reporter.* With no other choice, I fish in my pocket for my wallet, and pull out a photograph of Cara.

"I did. But the flashback was only part of the reason why." I hand her the photo and watch her eyes widen. "This is a picture of my wife from a week before her death."

She looks at it, then back at me, understanding dawning. "Oh my God."

6
CHAPTER SIX

Bethany

He says to call him Henry. He explains that in his daze he mistook me for his dead wife. Then he hands me the proof, and my attraction to him takes the weirdest twist possible.

I STARE AT THE SMILING, dead stranger in the photograph, and I see my own face. Cara Frakes looked so much like me that she could have been my older sister. Hell, she could have been my twin, were it not for face shape and the shades of our eyes.

THAT'S JUST CRAZY. The poor guy must have been questioning his own sanity the whole time. "Was she...from around here?" I ask slowly, my voice a little high with disbelief.

. . .

"Born and bred in the Adirondacks. Got...Got any cousins who resemble you at all?" He swallows, and as I look up at him I see how troubled his eyes are.

Of course. *This has to be a sore subject for him.* "Maybe. My Mom's whole family is from around here."

"Well," he says in a calmer voice with trickles of greater warmth, "They do bring up some beautiful women in the Adirondacks then."

I blush as I hand him back the photograph. I'm actually glad for the digression into flirting. *This is just too weird.* "Well, thank you. Twice, now."

His eyes twinkle. "No problem."

He brings me a toasted calzone along with a cup of coffee, then goes to grab his own. The farmhouse table I'm sitting at has an acre of blond oak as its top, and spindle legs as thick as my calf. He seems to love big, old, robust furniture and decor, giving even the prettiest painting or bit of stained glass a masculine cast.

It's him—in more ways than one. Apparently he made or refurbished almost everything in here. It seems to be a theme with him: rescuing the endangered, fixing the broken. The problem is...he seems a little broken himself.

. . .

WE EAT QUIETLY for a few minutes. I'm trying to remember the last time I reveled in this much melted cheese in front of a guy I'm attracted to, and I can't. But instead of looking at me in disgust or nagging me, Henry just smiles wistfully at me now and again as he eats like he's been working in the cold all day.

"SO YOU'RE A JOURNALISM INTERN? WHERE?" He wipes his mouth on a napkin, his big hands moving almost daintily.

"THE *TIMES*." I fight down a proud smile as his eyebrows rise. I wanted to crow from the rooftops when I got the internship, but right now, in front of this wealthy but modest man, I feel obliged to downplay my accomplishments.

"WOW. Wait, and you're how old?"

I BLUSH down to the roots of my hair. "I'm nineteen." *That's legal at least?* "I tested out of High School at sixteen, completed Junior College eighteen months later, and am at Cornell with a Communication major and the internship. I also have a local news blog."

"THAT'S A LOT OF ACCOMPLISHMENTS. And I should be focused on them, and not the fact that you're nineteen, but uh..." He lets out an awkward laugh. "Damn. Guess that makes me a dirty old man," he mumbles and I giggle and relax some.

. . .

The calzone is rich and filling, perfect after a long, chilly drive. He brews his coffee strong. "So I wasn't imposing on you by showing up uninvited, was I?" I ask between sips.

I probably was. But I should bring it up instead of just letting it slide in the face of such a weird situation.

"Well...I don't get many guests. My uncle comes up from his cottage for a while every day, and we have staff come in a few times a week to help keep the place up, especially the, uh, gardens." The corners of his eyes crinkle slightly. "Not that there's much to see out there yet."

"That's okay, I'm not here reporting on how late spring is coming this year. Though it is pretty crazy." The small talk sounds hollow in my mouth, and I shake my head. "I'm sorry."

"About what?" He gives me a curious look as he takes another bite of calzone.

"That...picture. Your wife." Cara Frakes died twenty years ago, the better part of a year before my birth. But that photo could have been taken of me yesterday.

He presses his lips together and looks out the window. "It hasn't been easy. Truth is, I'm glad you showed up. The way I was acting must have been very confusing, and I..."

. . .

"Hey," I broke in, sensing the grief lowering over his mood like a storm cloud. My crush on him has only intensified on discovering his sad secret and the bizarre mystery surrounding it. This handsome, powerful older man's vulnerability makes him approachable…and the strange circumstances make him even more fascinating.

He looks up, and I take a deep breath and plow on. "It's okay. Look, everyone's carrying something that messes with them. I am too."

He smiles tightly…but then his eyes search my face again. "Yeah, I uh…I noticed the bruise on your face. It wasn't from the crash, was it?"

I freeze. *Shit.* I did not realize that in his haze he would still remember every detail of my face. Including the mark that Michael left.

"I had a boyfriend. He had to go. He got violent when I kicked him out. He's kind of a problem now, which is why I left town for the weekend." It comes out in a rush, as if I'm trying to balance knowing his uncomfortable secret by sharing my own.

His reaction startles me. He doesn't just wince in sympathy; he sets his fork down, stiffening, a flash of unmistakable anger in his eyes. "Goddamn, I hate guys like that. Is he in jail?"

. . .

"Yeah, but his mother always bails him out when he screws up. He keeps calling me from different phone numbers, keeps showing up on my doorstep, the whole nine yards." I force a smile—and am shocked by the sad look of sympathy in his eyes.

"I take it he's the type to ignore protection orders," Henry sighs, and I nod.

"You guessed right." I look down into my coffee, suddenly feeling far too sober for this conversation. "You got any Irish we can put in this coffee?"

He lifts an eyebrow. "You suddenly turn twenty-one while I wasn't looking?"

I eye him. "Last week Michael punched me in the face. Then when I got away I nearly died in an avalanche and you had to rescue me. Today I discover that I'm your late wife's virtual twin." Then I soften, and brace myself.

Am I doing this? I'm doing this. I'm tired of being so timid that I never get what I want. "Which is extra awkward because half the reason I came up here was to find out if you're still single."

He blinks as if I just reached across and honked his nose, and then gets up from his chair. "I'll, uh, get the bottle of Bailey's."

. . .

"So I'll make you a deal. I'll tell you my story, and you tell me your story, and maybe we can sort out how to handle all the weird crap that's happened." He tops off my coffee mug with a shot or so of Bailey's and does the same to his mug.

"Okay, shoot." I don't want to tell him that I actually don't have much experience with alcohol outside of the occasional beer. But I just can't think about Michael any more, and Henry wants to know what's going on.

"I came from a working class family from Buffalo. Dad was a truck driver, Mom taught school. My uncle took me in after they died and raised me.

"Cara was my high school sweetheart. I was crazy for her. I wanted to make my fortunes so I could be a good husband to her. So I started buying and selling stuff on-line. Only problem was, most of the stuff I ended up buying and selling fell off a delivery truck or got stolen from a warehouse."

I stare at him, stunned by this sudden confession. He is basically telling me that he used to operate an on-line fence. It's more than shocking—it's reckless. And I know he's only trusting me with his secrets because I'm wearing his dead wife's face.

"How did you find out?" The reporter in me is kicking in, my curiosity driving me to pry deeper instead of telling him that he's giving me, a stranger, too much information.

"I was asked to have a large number of diamonds re-cut and

sold, and the supplier and I would split the profits. I didn't realize that the Antwerp Diamond Exchange had just been hit by a massive robbery. But I put two and two together.

"I HAD ALREADY MADE enough to fund all the legitimate investments that I would need to support us. So I decided to get out of the business, and propose to Cara as an hones man. We were very young—nineteen, in fact, and I was already done with my wild youth." He looks wistfully out the window and sips his drink.

"BUT CARA WAS VERY SMART, like you. She didn't miss much. She figured out that my stories about where I got my investment money didn't add up." His confession goes on, almost unbearably, and I gulp my coffee, feeling a faint blush of warmth starting almost at once from the liquor.

"SHE FOUND out the truth and got angry at you?" I wonder if I would too. I can certainly understand doing some shady things in your desperate days. I'm still in mine, after all. But running some kind of on-line, Deep Web fence seems a little wild even by my standards.

"FURIOUS. She wouldn't tell me what was wrong for days, and then she sprung it on me when she was irritated at me during the last leg of a long drive home." He drains his mug, fills it three quarters full of coffee from the carafe, and fills the rest up with Bailey's.

. . .

"What happened then?" I think I know, and it makes me sick to my stomach even while I crave the comforting warmth of more Bailey's.

"She died," he mumbles, staring into his mug. "We argued, I got distracted, a drunk driver drifted over into our lane, and by the time I saw him, I couldn't stop in time on the icy road. She uh, wasn't...wearing a seatbelt."

I can't help it then. I reach over and put my much smaller hand over his huge, callused one. "I'm sorry. That sounds like Hell."

"That's a glimpse of it here on Earth," he agrees. "And it isn't your fault that the way we met stirred all that up."

"It's still weird as Hell," I mutter, and he nods. I wonder, right then, if this will get in the way of us being...anything...to each other. It may be too painful for him. And me?

How will I ever know for sure that he wants me, and not me as a stand-in for...her?

The sudden, urgent question worries me...but it doesn't put a dent in my attraction to Henry. I'm too far gone, even as I realize how messed up that is.

. . .

"I THINK I'd like a second drink," I say quietly.

HE EYES my mug and then the bottle. "You sure?"

I THINK about going over the mess with Michael as my half of this weird quid-pro-quo, and wince, nodding. "Oh yeah."

CHAPTER SEVEN

Henry

I end up carrying poor Bethany to bed not two hours later.

IT'S A FUN TWO HOURS. We talk about her crazy ex, his antics so far, and how she had to tell security at work about him yesterday. How persistent he is; how he seems to be escalating, and doesn't even seem to understand that he already killed their relationship with his fists.

HER PHONE BEEPS in the middle of our conversation, and she checks it. Multiple messages from another number. She listens to the first two seconds of one, winces, and shuts her phone off. "It's him, he's out of jail and just said he's coming over."

. . .

"Does he know what hotel you're staying in?" I try to keep my voice calm, and ignore the urge to find this miserable boy and beat on him until he agrees to leave Bethany alone forever.

"No...no." She pushes her hair out of slightly reddened eyes. "He has no idea that I'm out of town."

"Good." I fold my arms. "Then you're safe for now. He can sit on your doorstep all damn weekend long, while you drink Bailey's and coffee and go skiing."

Her smile comes back tentatively, and she tucks her phone back in her pocket. "Maybe I'll get lucky and he'll freeze."

"That's the spirit!"

Exhaustion and too much Bailey's have her nodding off on my couch as we talk about our lives and interests. I take one look at her and insist that she take the spare room instead of driving home. I ignore the instant boner I get at the prospect of her sleeping under the same roof as I, even innocently.

So I carry her to bed, teasing her gently about her lack of an alcohol tolerance while she blushes and giggles sleepily. She's adorable, and I am hard as a rock. But she is also too close to drunk, and a young stranger, and things between us are...complicated.

I tuck her in instead of joining her, and resist the urge to kiss her goodnight when she sleepily offers. But it takes me all of my self-control.

Gonna do the right thing, *damn it, even if it leaves my balls aching.* Which it does. But I don't mind; the low-level burn of frustration reminds me that I'm a man, with urges that would be a deep pleasure to finally satisfy.

My uncle, surprisingly, makes himself scarce all night. I think he knows I have someone over, though he's likely miles off from the truth in his suspicions. *I'm going to have a Hell of a time explaining this to him,* I think as I drink enough water to counter the Bailey's and start preparing for bed.

It takes all my strength of will not to go back and watch Bethany sleep. The longing is natural; I fell asleep to that face for two precious years. But that face belongs to a new friend now, not an old lover.

I resolutely go straight to sleep instead.

"Cara? Cara, are you all right?"

We're on our side in a ditch. I lost count of how many times we rolled trying to avoid that damned drunk driver. I'm wrenched and sore and dizzy, but my seatbelt held.

. . .

Cara, though, hates seatbelts since she got pregnant. She says they rub against her tender boobs and make them sore. Now she's slumped against the shattered dashboard with little cubes of broken glass all around her.

She isn't moving. Not one inch. I reach over and brush the broken glass off her back, and touch something sticky. Blood. Not flowing blood...drying blood. Her body feels stiff and wrong under my hand.

"Cara?!?"

The note of panic in my voice is so raw and vulnerable that hearing it deepens my helplessness as I take her pulse and find nothing. I pull her back, trying to start CPR—and look into her bloody face and staring eyes.

"Cara...no, baby. No. Come on, please...no..."

Begging becomes weeping and pleading, and weeping and pleading becomes screaming. And I scream myself awake that way, tears in my eyes and my throat and heart both raw.

Fifteen seconds later, my door bangs open suddenly. I expect to see my uncle but instead, a smaller, curvy figure hurries in, shutting the door behind her. I smell musky perfume as she draws near. "Hey," comes the worried voice in the dark. "Are you okay?"

Right then, my usually tough, capable ass feels about as tough and capable as a terrified kid. The moment of losing Cara is still echoing in my head like a gunshot. I wrap my arms around the woman at my bedside and bury my face in her belly.

She goes still for a moment, and then her arms go around me. "Hey, it's okay," she murmurs soothingly as I hang on for dear life. "It's okay."

This is Bethany, I remember dimly as I nestle my face against her soft, warm body. But my own body reacts anyway, relaxing as she strokes my hair. A surge of desire runs through me, banishing the darkness inside like a torch being lit.

I clutch her hips and pull her closer.

CHAPTER EIGHT

Bethany

I gasp slightly as Henry pulls me close. The gesture is so desperate that for a harrowing moment I worry that he's half awake and thinks I'm his wife again. I want him to be embracing me—not her—and I shiver and hug him tighter. "It's Bethany. Are you all right?"

"Flashback," he manages, and I nod and just hug him. He seems oriented, but I'm not sure.

After a few moments, I relax and nuzzle his hair, breathing in his woodsmoke-and-coffee scent mixing with the masculine musk of his sweat. I've wanted to be in his arms for over a week...but not like this. The pleasure of having his strong arms around me is a guilty one; it feels like something stolen.

He hangs onto me for a minute, shaking, and then relaxes his grip, lifting his head. I can see the dim outlines of his face in the light from the hallway, but I can't make out his expression. Then his big hand cups the back of my head, gripping my ponytail with a gentle firmness that sends tingles through me.

"I'm okay now," he murmurs, the shaky, distracted tone gone. "Now that you're here."

The purr in his voice makes me weak in the knees.

"So now what do we...do?" I murmur as I look up at him.

"I can think of a few things," he says softly as he leans close, the last word spoken right against my lips.

We kiss, and it sends a flush of warmth through me, tightening my nipples and making my heart beat hard. He feels so good; his hot mouth on mine makes me swoon. His powerful arms hold me against him securely; he both cradles me and controls me at once.

My response is daring; more daring than I'm used to being. But there's no way that I'm chickening out and missing my chance. I want the taste of Michael out of my mouth and the feel of him off of my body. And if the hottest man I have ever met is volunteering...

I tug the spaghetti straps of my dark blue silk nightgown off my shoulders, and let the gown slither slowly down my body as his eyes widen in surprised delight. "Me too," I breathe, trying to ignore how my heart is pounding in my ears.

Fuck you, Michael. This is how I get my revenge. By screwing an amazing guy in his castle of a house while you freeze your ass off on my porch or in a jail cell. I will forget everything about you, Michael, especially your mediocre fucking. I will replace those memories with him.

Henry draws me forward into the warm, soft space under the blankets, and I go willingly, hungry for his touch.

His big, hard body shivers slightly as I lie down over him. I can feel his erection digging into my belly through his thin silk sleeping shorts. I wrap my arms around him and lay my head on his shoulder, drowsy contentment and a deep sense of safety mixing with my growing desire.

I press my breasts against his powerful chest and feel his

heartbeat pick up. "My dreams were shitty too," I murmur against his mouth. "Let's distract each other."

We kiss, slow and sweet, while one of his hands controls my head and the other eagerly explores me. His warm, callused hand runs over my skin, managing to soothe me and set my skin tingling with excitement at the same time. I feel my nipples tighten against his chest, and rub my body against him sensually while he lets out a soft groan.

"Bethany," he murmurs worshipfully, and hearing the sound of my name reassures me and turns me on even more. Then both his hands start exploring me, and I melt against him, running my hands up through his hair as he starts kissing my neck.

From the way he's shuddering as we caress each other, he wants it just as badly as I do. But in spite of this, he takes his time. I feel his fingers everywhere: sliding down my back, kneading my ass, tracing the crease that runs down from my hip and becomes the top inside of my thigh.

His hands are firm and knowing, and he pays attention, finding the spots to caress that make me whimper instead of greedily grabbing for what interests him most. His thumbs slide back and forth over my nipples, trace the lines of my throat and the curves of my ass; then his kisses intensify, and he starts using his tongue as well.

He sits up as I straddle his lap, bending me back as he runs his tongue in a long, tingling trail back and forth over my chest. Then his tongue tip starts tracing over my breast: swirling inward, slowly, taking his time while I start to shiver and pant.

"Don't stop," I whisper, and he looks up at me with a dark flame burning in the backs of his eyes.

"Not unless you beg," he growls, and I feel it down to my toes.

I'm not used to pleasure during sex. He must have figured

that out. The way I can't control my movements or noise; the gasps and whimpers at every new caress.

Sex for me has been a nice thing to do for someone else, at best; a humiliating chore, at worst. Now, I want it, in an unfamiliar, selfish way.

He bends me back a little further, and sucks one of my nipples into his mouth. My mind goes blank at once. "Ah!" I cry, and he responds with another hard pull.

I don't know what to do. I squirm; my head falls back, and my hands flutter in midair at his shoulders as he sucks greedily. I'm fighting not to push his face away from my breast but it feels too good…I can't take it.

His hands catch my wrists suddenly; I struggle against them reflexively as he starts lashing his tongue against my trapped nipple. I strain in his grip, anger and gratitude mixing with my lust as he forces me to accept the pleasure. My whole pussy starts to ache and tingle as he holds me steady—until I get too turned on to fight.

I hear him starting to pant and groan against my breast and realize that I'm grinding my pussy against him slowly every time he draws on my nipple. The movement draws the silk against his trapped cock.

I grin, my hands lowering to his shoulders to brace me as he lets me go. Then I bear down, and grind on him harder.

He pulls hard enough to take me to the edge of pain; my body goes taut and I let out a wail. His hands are kneading my ass now, roughly digging his fingers against the muscle and sending jolts of pleasure through my hips. He lets my nipple go —and fastens roughly onto the other, making me rock against him even more frantically.

I'm starting to need his cock in me. It's not a sensation I'm used to; I can't remember the last time I wanted a man to fuck me so badly that it hurt. But now, I can feel the ache of his absence like sexual hunger pangs.

One of his hands wanders over my hip, and then slides around to cup my pussy and squeeze it firmly. I gasp, grinding harder in response, pushing my swollen clit against the heel of his hand. He starts kneading me, rolling that part of his hand against me and sending a hard jolt of pleasure through me with each push.

My toes curl; my back arches, and my head falls back as I struggle for air. I've never felt this much physical pleasure in my life, and I know that if I pull away he'll hold me firm and make me take it.

The idea delights me. Shyness can't win. Inexperience can't win. Fear of losing control and humiliating myself can't win either. His hand, his tongue, his will—he's going to get me there, even if I fight him on instinct.

Oh yes. Don't stop. Fuck me...push me past all this shyness...make me scream.

My whole body lights up at his touch; sweat gathers on my skin, and my pussy feels ready to start giving off steam. My nipples hurt from hardness; he's marking my neck now instead, sucking hard, teeth scraping me delightfully.

He slides a finger in between my labia and starts stroking my clit; I seize up, heart pounding in my ears as my pussy aches, tightening around nothing. My hips rock harder, making him grunt.

"I need..." I whimper. "I need...you..."

He groans against my neck again and then lifts his head. "Bedside...drawer. Condoms."

Well, that's responsible of him.

I sit up on my knees so he can shuck off his sleep shorts. He yanks them down eagerly—and a shock clears some of the sex-haze from my head at once. *Wow.*

I blink down at the biggest, thickest cock I have seen in my life and realize that I may have overestimated how much I can handle. *Holy shit that is one serious tool.* I can't even fit one hand around it; a little intimidated, I feel doubt mix with my lust...and then float away again as I stroke it and he shudders and lets out a groan.

Big, but sensitive. I could play with it all day. But how the hell do I fit it inside me?

This is going to take planning...and more than a little courage. I buy time by fishing in his bedside drawer and finding a lubricated condom, then unwrapping it and rolling it onto him. He squirms slightly, lifting his hips, and I feel his cock throb so hard with anticipation that it knocks lightly against my palm.

I'm not about to chicken out now. I go up on my knees and straddle him, taking his cock in hand. I fit the thick head inside of me and close my eyes, settling over it slowly.

He pants, strain deepening on his face as I gradually stuff myself with the beast he's been hiding in those shorts. It hurts and arouses me at once, just like the light pain of his firm grip tightening on my hips until his fingertips dig into me.

Has it really been twenty years? I settle another inch and his eyes fly open, a delirious cry bursting from his lips as he visibly fights to keep from thrusting up into me.

"Yes," he shouts. "Yes!"

...And suddenly I can believe it. My first good sex ever; his first at all in longer than I have been alive. I grin and force myself down another inch. Then another.

My muscles tighten around him uncomfortably as I struggle to get used to his girth. I'm still too turned on to care that much about hurting myself a little. In fact, the pain as I slide down puts a glorious edge on my pleasure that intensifies it more.

And the look on his face...for that I would suffer a little even if it didn't feel good. He trembles as I work my way down, and his finger starts swirling against my clit in a way that makes me start trembling too.

I push down further, feeling like I'm mounting something endlessly long. Yet even as I force myself to slowly take him in, I feel my excitement growing. He never stops pleasuring me, no matter how hard I work my body against his cock as I move downward.

We're both moaning and writhing by the time I settle over him fully; I can feel the pain going away as that finger stroking me starts to feel better and better. He's holding the small of my back with his other hand, watching me intently as I whimper and ride him reflexively.

I stare back at him, astonished, excited, enthralled, as every cell in my body starts to shimmer with pleasure. Then I can't any more; my eyes roll closed, and I rock against him wildly, my cries going more and more desperate.

"Come on, now, sweetheart. Let go for me. Be a good girl," he purrs in my ear, and I can't take any more at all.

I scream. An expanding sphere of pure ecstasy explodes outward from my clit and takes over entirely, making me thrash with pleasure. It's stronger than I ever imagined, electrifying my whole body and shutting my shyness down completely.

I ride him roughly, grinding against his cock and his finger to keep the spasms of delight going for as long as I can.

He keeps moving his hand, merciless, and I keep squirming and contracting and crying out as I ride him. It goes on and on —until suddenly he stiffens and starts to shout with each breath.

Practically limp from exhaustion, I force myself to keep grinding away as his voice grows louder and hoarser. His hips lift, pushing his cock deep into me—and then I feel it jolt and shudder as he groans with joy.

"Aaah! Ah—Bethany! Oh...oh..." His voice lowers to a contented rumble, and he relaxes under me. "...Oh, yeah."

I collapse onto his chest, into his arms, the last of my strength spent in bringing him off. He cradles me, and strokes my hair as I lie there stunned.

"Bethany. Such a good, lovely girl. I may have to keep you."

I smile as I drift off.

CHAPTER NINE

Henry

I wake slowly after hours of peaceful sleep, to feel a familiar warm body curled against my side. My cock wakes almost at once, rising against my belly as I roll over to stroke her hair aside and look down at my lover.

...And then I remember.

I freeze, torn between lying back down and leaping away from her out of the bed entirely. *Bethany. This is Bethany.*

I remember fucking her last night. I remember her trembling and thrashing under me as she came. The tears on her cheeks as she admitted she had never been brought to climax before. How I kissed them away...and then made her experience that same pleasure again and again.

No. I knew it was Bethany. I knew. Cara wasn't pre-orgasmic. I knew who I was fucking the whole time.

I'm not that crazy. Really.

I relax and lie back down beside her, gazing at her fondly. *Maybe I'm over-thinking all of this. Yes, she looks an awful lot like Cara, but she's not Cara. Maybe I just have a "type".*

Maybe it's okay.

I've spent twenty years blaming myself for Cara's death, and second-guessing myself because of the head-space that the PTSD left me in. Maybe it's time to stop. Maybe it's time to stop acting like I've been frozen in place for twenty years, when I know I've gotten better over time.

I run a hand down her bare back; she shivers and rolls toward me, and I wrap an arm around her. Her own dreams don't always seem kind either. Maybe I can help her with them, just as she rushed to comfort me when my own made me scream myself awake.

I don't worry about her judging me. But with her walking around wearing Cara's face, how can I get her to trust that I want her, and not who she looks like?

The only answer I can come up with is to learn her wants and needs, and use them to spoil her completely...and specifically. It might not be everything that I need to be doing to keep this new fire going. But as I bury my nose in her hair, I think to myself that it's a damn good place to start.

I move closer to her, sliding down her body a little so that my head is level with those glorious breasts of hers. She's just a touch curvier than Cara, her nipples darker and more sensitive. I kiss them gently, and she whimpers and squirms sleepily against the bedding. Her thigh slides against mine, and I feel her nipple tighten against my lips.

She moans as I suckle delicately at each of her breasts in turn, going slow, ignoring my erection's pounding urgency again. Last night has only left me thirsty to sink my cock deep into her again...but that can wait.

I feel her hand slide up my back...and she lets out a soft sigh of pleasure. "Henry," she whispers. "Mm...don't stop." And her fingers tangle in my hair again.

There are a million things I want to try on her, if I can get her to return soon—or better yet, stay longer. I'm into a lot of experimentation...I even have a few scars from playing a bit too rough.

I'm proud of them. I love it when I pleasure a woman so well that she loses control and hurts me a little. And I know that last night, Bethany felt the same way when I left little finger-bruises on her back.

Twenty pent-up years exploded out of me in that moment...and now, I just want more. More sex, more pleasure...more Bethany. I slide my hands down her sides and over her hips as I suckle light and slow, and she starts to croon in time to the pulls of my mouth.

One of my hands pinches her labia lightly between two fingers and tugs and strokes it, teasing her further. Her moans change pitch, and she starts to buck her hips against my hand. My other hand slides up to rub and tease her ass, just pressing my thumb against her back opening without entering.

"Unh!" she cries out, lifting her hips against my hand aggressively. Her hips roll; I hear a pleading note in her whimpers, and just keep on teasing her until she uses her words. "I need your cock," she pants finally. "Please."

"Are you going to take it like a good girl this time, all in one go?" My erection aches for her more with every heartbeat; I'm so dizzy that between lust and sleepiness I can barely think. I feel like I'm going to explode if I don't fuck her soon. But I keep my voice calm, and in control.

"Yes," she whimpers. "Yes, yes, I'll be good, please..."

I settle between her thighs eagerly, and sink the head of my cock into her. Somehow it feels even better than last night, her delicate folds caressing my shaft as I slide past them. Her hot, slick passage tightens around me, embracing me from every side as I thrust in deeper.

"That's it," I groan. "That's it, sweetheart, take it..." She whimpers, and I start stroking her clit directly, turning the high sound into a throaty moan. "Good girl, good girl."

"It's...I...I...it's too much..." Her voice rises into a wail. "It's too good—"

"Keep going. Take it all. Almost there." I keep stroking her clit softly, and lean down to suckle at her breast again.

She digs her nails into my ass and presses up against me, another sobbing moan vibrating her throat as I slide the rest of the way into her. *"Henry..."*

"There. Oh, there." My back arches; I pant, fighting the urge to thrust fast and blast off right away. We hold still together, trembling, both doing our best not to climax yet.

When the tension ebbs away enough, I start grinding against her slowly, my thumb circling over her clit as I move. "Good girl. You feel so good, baby."

Her pussy feels incredible. I can feel every bit of it, even her cervix rubbing softly against the tip of my cock when I go in deep enough. The sensation is so exquisite that I groan aloud again, my whispered orders turning into animal sounds of pleasure.

Holy shit, what brand of condoms is this? I need a case or twelve. I thrust in again—and feel her muscles tighten around me. She's gasping and sobbing, shimmying against me, and I feel the last bit of my rational mind start to shut down.

I let go a little and start fucking her in faster, sharper thrusts, grunting and shouting over her cries as she lifts her hips to meet mine. For long, delightful minutes we draw closer and closer to the edge together...and I can't remember when I felt such bliss.

*So good...so good...so good...*It takes every ounce of self-control I have to keep stroking her clit as she squirms and bucks under me. I slow my hips further, wanting to savor the amazing sensation...even as she starts to shake and dig her nails into me hard.

"More," she sobs. "More, more, *please more...*"

Oh well. "Oh, Bethany," I purr—and start fucking her harder.

"Ah...ah...yes, just like that, don't stop!" Her nails sting me deliciously as her begging and trembling excite me even more. I thrust faster, barely noticing the nagging doubt still lingering in the back of my head.

And then, in the middle of the frenzy, as she's clawing stripes into my ass and wrapping her legs hard around me and bucking under me for all she is worth, it suddenly hits me.

I forgot the fucking condom.

I freeze, gathering the will to force myself out of her sweet pussy and not come back until my cock is properly dressed. But it's far too late.

"Ah! Ah! Oh, oh Henry—I'm coming!" She clings to me with all four limbs, pumping and grinding against me wildly—and then wails as she presses up hard against me and her muscles start milking my shaft.

It's too good. My balls tighten as the pressure in me races toward explosion. *Oh no—!*

"Oh *yes!*" I hear myself roar as my bare cock spasms inside of her. My panting shouts join with hers as my cum jets again and again into her hot, trembling body. My mind goes blank; her contractions suck every last drop out of me, and with it all my strength.

I collapse into her arms, shaking, almost shocked by the power of that climax. I can feel little spasms run through her flesh, caressing my hypersensitive shaft and making me gasp for air. It's amazing. She's amazing.

"Yes," I whisper, wondering how in the hell I lived without *this* for so long. "Oh, yes."

I'm supposed to be telling her something, I think dimly as she pets my hair and shoulders. But instead, I'm drifting off. The worry nagging at me just got blown right out of my head.

"Bethany," I murmur into her shoulder, and feel her relax a little more as we both start to fall asleep.

I don't remember what was bothering me all the rest of Saturday, as we eat and make love, and use my hot tub and make love, and take hikes in the woods. We use condoms, and I pleasure her each time until I lose my strength and she loses consciousness. We watch bad science fiction movies, and laugh at them, and then forget them as we make out like horny teens on the couch.

Only at the end of the weekend, as she starts her drive home early Sunday afternoon, do I remember. As I watch her slightly battered little car drive back down the mountain, that awkward just-pre-orgasmic memory comes back to me in a sudden rush, and I curse under my breath.

Damn it! I didn't mean to do that. She's going to be upset. More upset, if I don't tell her promptly.

I'll tell her soon. Once she's settled back home. I wanted to invite her back next weekend anyway. I know I'm clean of any diseases, at least.

I'll just...tell her I found a rip in one of the condoms. That could happen to anyone. Better that than let her know that twenty years of thirst had me make a dumbass mistake like a sex-addled teenager.

I feel a tentative smile creep back onto my face. *We can sort this out.*

Of course, it's easy to believe in a happy ending when the princess you want has been fucking you all weekend. I only hope that my optimism isn't misplaced.

CHAPTER TEN

Bethany

"So how was it?" My therapist sits forward, dark eyes bright with interest and a gleeful little smile on her face.

"He was amazing," I gush before I can stop myself, and she laughs. "No, seriously, I've never felt anything like that before. He was..." I hesitate, searching for words. "I felt a real connection."

"Well, I'm hoping that's not all you felt after all that build-up," she laughs.

I laugh along, and then shake my head as I catch my breath.

"No. No, it wasn't, but never mind that. I just...he was..." I start giggling then, and bury my face in my hands, unable to stop.

She watches me, patient. Finally I catch my breath again. "I'm sorry, seriously. I just really like this guy."

"I noticed. I've never seen you this happy over anyone ever. Certainly not Michael." There's a faint edge in her voice; she's said over and over how proud she is of me for standing firm as he keeps trying to push his way back into my life.

"Michael was...a mistake. Henry has some problems, and he is older than me, but it's not like Michael. Michael used pity to edge his way living off my money, and then once he had what he wanted he turned into a childish little dick. Henry...Henry's just hurting."

"Hurting how?"

I feel a sudden flare of self-consciousness at her pointed little question. Somewhere between the lines I can see the real question. *Bethany, honey, you told me yourself that Henry is struggling with even more trauma and depression than you, and that his trauma centers on the loss of his wife.*

The wife that you look like. The wife that you're worried he keeps mistaking you for when his grasp on reality slips a little. The wife that you don't want to be just a stand-in for.

"He's got PTSD from the loss of his wife. The accident. It got triggered again by the avalanche.

"But even though he was struggling, he still dug me out of a car before he knew who I was or what I looked like. That's the kind of guy he is." And maybe I'm hero-worshiping him a little but, but it was my life that he saved.

She gives me her warmest smile. "Well, I think that you're definitely trading up. And you could use an excuse to get out of town more weekends. I know how hard you work. So why not have a little fun with your handsome widower friend?"

I drive home with a light heart. My doubts about Henry have mostly burned away in the heat of that incredible weekend, and having my therapist cheering me on really helps. I am definitely going back up to see him next weekend, for more of that awesome sex, and the best company I've had in...I don't even know when.

The doubts that still linger...well, those will take time. He said my name in bed, not hers; he must have known that that was me, and not Cara. But I still remember how he acted when we first met.

I'm praying that it's me he wants. Not just my resemblance to her.

I'm thinking about suggesting a barbecue now that things are warming up a little in the Adirondacks. I'm going to miss skiing this season, but that's all right. I have something better—something that I have waited for a hell of a lot longer.

I'M SMILING as I turn the corner onto my block—and then my expression freezes and my eyes widen. Six cop cars and two fire trucks are pulled up in front of my apartment building...and there's smoke pouring out of the lobby.

I PARK HALF a block behind the emergency vehicles and approach slowly, hugging my thick alpaca shawl around myself as I stare at the drama unfolding head of me. Confusion and shock give way to growing horror as I hear familiar yelling: a young male voice gone hoarse from the fit he's throwing.

"OH GOD," I mumble as I hurry forward, shoving my way up to the barricade.

MICHAEL IS FIGHTING four cops as they drag him out of the smoke and down the apartment stairs. He's struggling and screaming, red-faced, eyes squinted with the same out-of-control tantrum-level rage and cheeks greased with tears. "No, no, no, you can't do this! You gotta let it burn!"

I DRAW BACK AWAY from the barricade and let some rubberneckers shove past me, providing me some camouflage as the cops drag him onto the sidewalk. He keeps ranting the whole time.

. . .

"That slut threw me out! She threw me out when I didn't do anything! You gotta let me get back at her, man, you gotta let it burn!"

They're shoving him toward one of the squad cars, his hands cuffed behind his back. His blond hair is askew and he has that same wild, flaily body language he had when he hit me.

He's crazy. I draw back further as his voice rises to high screeching, not even words any more. My heart is pounding with terror. *He's irrational and dangerous. And it scares the shit out of me.*

A car door slams on his screams and I let out a sob. I draw away, knowing someone among the cops will be calling me soon, and not wanting to be caught in the crowd when my phone goes off. I can't deal with a face to face with the police until I stop feeling like I'm going to throw up.

Why is he like this? Why did I miss that he is like this? What if I make the same mistake with Henry, whom I already know has problems?

What happens when the honeymoon period ends with him too? Who will I end up with?

My eyes fill with tears and I hurry off, headed for my neighborhood coffee shop to pull myself together.

. . .

THE POLICE CALL while I'm deep in a double chocolate mocha, the rest of which grows cold as I get the details.

MICHAEL CAME to burn my building down, since he couldn't get at me directly. When the security guard they had hired for the lobby wouldn't let him past, he set the fire right there. It didn't burn more than a supply closet, and the guard restrained him and called the cops.

I CONFIRM my order of protection, the assault charges and Michael's multiple violations. They ask if I'm able to move somewhere else before he's released on bail. I think about the savings I've depleted, my lack of friends in town, and how much I'm starting to hate Boston. And I say yes before I even know for sure, just to get them to finish up with me.

I FINISH MY COLD MOCHA. I want so much to go home and hide in my bed. But my home, that pretty little apartment I worked so hard to keep, suddenly isn't home any more. At least for now.

MAYBE FOREVER. I no longer feel safe there.

I PLAN on calling my therapist when I pull out my phone again. But I don't make the call. I set the phone down on the table in front of me, and pick at my sandwich and salad.

. . .

I've had it with fixers. Henry might be hurting but at least he's made a life for himself—not to mention, saved mine. But what the hell is with Michael? What did he think would happen once he put his damn hands on me?

But I know. Because he thinks I deserved to be hit. Because he thinks that he was just putting me in my place.

Just like he was completely okay with setting my apartment building on fire, hurting a lot of people just to punish me.

He's not just a sexist, not just an immature little bully, not just the world's worst case of arrested development. He's not living in the same reality as the rest of us. He's walking around in his own, thinking that because he feels something strongly, he can disregard law, and decency, and everyone else in the world.

And I let him fuck me for over a year.

I blink tears away, hating whatever self-destructive part of me let things get this far. I know that most of it was his manipulation, and his constant breaking of my trust. But I was the one who avoided dealing with this until it reached the breaking point, because I was that scared of confrontation.

Maybe something in me sensed that he would end up flipping out on me. But the thing that is getting me is...what if Henry is also more unstable than I think? What if good sex is fucking up my judgment?

I FINALLY GIVE up and call him. I have gas money but not enough cash for a room, and no credit card. I hate being young, broke and desperate; I hate having to ask a guy I've just barely become lovers with for help.

BUT I HATE EVEN MORE the idea of going back to my apartment while it still stinks of Michael's arson, and reminds me of him, and feels unsafe. I hate having to face my neighbors, and pray that none of them make the connection between me and the lunatic who tried to burn down all our homes. I just want to get away again, from Boston and all its problems, back to the arms of the one guy in a very long time who makes me feel safe.

AND YET IT still takes me fifteen minutes and three tries to actually put in his number and connect the call.

HENRY PICKS up after two rings. He's panting. "Hey."

"HENRY...? I GOTTA TALK TO YOU." I can't keep the fear out of my voice.

I HEAR A CREAK AND A CLANG, like gym equipment. His voice goes serious. "Is this about this weekend?"

. . .

"I—wait, what about this weekend?" I'm confused now. "I thought we had a good time." I can suddenly smell another unexpected problem on the wind; it makes me skittish.

"Well I figured you must have run into some kind of related...issue. I mean, it's too soon to tell on your end, I'm guessing, but maybe I'm wrong. Is it about that?" He sounds...guilty. And a little hazy again.

What the hell is this now? Alarm bells are going off in my head. "Is it about what? Henry, you're being vague as Hell—what are you talking about?"

"I...look," he ventures. "I'm sorry, but before you say anything, I know I fucked up. I should have just called you as soon as I found out, but I was trying to figure out what to say."

My chest hurts from my heart beating so hard. "What to say about what?"

"Uh...I discovered when I was cleaning up that one of the condoms broke."

I freeze, blinking slowly. "...What?"

He goes on like this is a normal conversation. "I'm clean of any

STDs or anything else communicable, so that's not an issue, but...I don't have a vasectomy."

He sounds very calm and apologetic, and I realize that he's waited to tell me this because he's been rehearsing it.

And somehow that makes me furious. So angry that I know I won't be keeping my voice down. I throw a dollar tip on the table, grab my bag and walk outside with the phone pressed to my ear. "How...long have you known?"

"Uh—just overnight," he says, and the guilt deepens in his voice. He said he knows he fucked up. But he doesn't seem to grasp just how much.

My free hand balls into a fist as I walk into the parking lot. I'm sick of irrational, irresponsible men adding to my goddamn problems when I can handle it least. "So let me get this straight," I say slowly in a quiet, light voice that has a volcano of rage rumbling away behind it.

"I call you scared to death by something completely fucking unrelated to this weekend, because I need help and don't really have anyone to turn to. And instead of listening and finding out what is up, you decide to unload this on me? After waiting an extra day to say anything about possibly getting me pregnant?

· · ·

There's a long silence on the other end of the line. I feel my anger crest again and fill it. "Michael tried to burn my apartment building down! And you want to dump the fact that you may have gotten me pregnant on me right fucking now?"

"I'm very sorry, Cara—"

A wave of fury roars through me and I scream into the phone. "What the *fuck* did you just call me?"

And I hang up.
 I stand there shaking, tears brimming over coldly in my eyes. *Oh God. I'm an idiot. I should never have trusted him.*

He loved fucking me because I look like her. He doesn't actually care about me. He flakes on telling me important things and calls me by his dead wife's name.

I'm not important to him—I'm just a stand-in!

I manage to get into my car before the damn breaks, but just barely. Then I lean over the wheel and sob.

My luck with men is just as bad as ever. I will always be alone.

CHAPTER ELEVEN

Henry

Uncle Jake gets a cursory explanation after he finds me sitting in the gym stunned with the phone still in my hand. Then I grab a bottle of Jack and disappear into my room.

Now and again I leave a message on Bethany's phone. I keep it short and stop calling after nine. The next day, I try again once it's late enough in the morning.

It tears me up that she won't pick up or call back. But she hasn't blocked me either. That doesn't keep me from loathing myself, however.

Jake lets me wallow in my guilt and misery for exactly one day before he comes banging on my door and hauls me out on a walk through the woods. He's brought his camera, not his gun, and leans on a walking stick as we hike up the mountain trail at the back side of my property.

I protest the whole way up the mountain. I'm nursing a hangover, haven't shaved, haven't slept or eaten. My stomach feels like it's been used as a sewer.

It's a perfect counterpoint to the gnawing, hollow pain in my chest. "What is this about?" I demand as Jake slows down to hand me one of the bottles of water he's brought along.

"Just keep walking and sipping on that. I'm trying to figure out how to bring this up without kicking your ass or calling you an idiot." He sounds tired and angry, and I can't really blame him. I'm angry at myself.

"Fine." I don't have to talk, or listen to him, to get a lecture about what a selfish, thoughtless idiot I was with Bethany. I have been doing that in my heart for thirty hours. That beautiful, sweet girl deserves so much better than a guy who hides from important conversations and fucks them up when he can't.

And even though it was just a slip in an emotional moment, I would have to be completely stupid not to realize why she was upset when I called her Cara.

We reach the lookout point at the top of the path, and I stand next to my uncle and look out over the misty mountainside. He takes a sip from his brandy flask, and then looks over at me without offering it. "That girl who looks like Cara. You found her, took her home and fucked her, didn't you?"

I wince. "No, she found me and showed up at our door."

He frowns. "Damn. I can't exactly yell at you for that part. But what the hell happened after that?"

I sigh and look down. "Things got out of hand."

"Out of hand how?" His tone is as hard as nails.

"Her name's Bethany. Looking me up, meeting me, drinking with me, staying over, sleeping with me...those were all her decisions, Jake." I can't keep a touch of defensiveness out of my voice.

"She did this knowing about Cara?" His eyes search my face, and I nod firmly. He relaxes slightly. "Okay, well, good that you at least got that part handled before you and she got into anything. But then what?"

I rub my face and look away. "I fucked up multiple times in quick succession when she needed me to be there for her, and now she won't return my calls."

He shakes his head. "Fuck." Then he shocks me by pulling out a cigarette and lighting it. He only smokes when he's under real stress, or has to chew something over especially hard.

"This girl...were you fucking her because it's easy to pretend she's Cara?"

His blunt question shocks me a little, but I can understand the reason behind it. "No. I feel guilty about fucking someone who isn't Cara. That part's true. And maybe there's a dumb little wishful thought in the back of my head that maybe Cara...reincarnated. Came back to me.

"But even if that were true, she wouldn't be Cara any more. This lifetime, she's Bethany."

He turns his head and blows smoke out over his shoulder. "A totally different woman, with her own needs, her own likes and dislikes. Who deserves to be loved for her, not as a stand-in for someone else."

"I'm too sober for this conversation," I admit, ears prickling.

"Shut the fuck up. You'll manage." He locks eyes with me. "You understand that even if people can come back like that, what I just said is still true. If you treat her like Cara, if you call her Cara, she will never believe that you love *her*."

I stare at him for a moment. "Bethany's special. She reminds me of Cara but that's not why I'm with her. I just have...a type. That's all."

"Well, you keep that in mind. However it is that this girl showed up in your life when she needed someone and so did you, you should be grateful for it and enjoy it. Not mess it up and reject it because you can't move on from your wife."

I scoff in tired amazement. "What is all of this about?"

"I had girlfriends after my wife died, you know," he says

slowly, and then pulls long and thoughtfully on his smoke. "Took me a while, but I did it. Great girls. I cared about them a lot and we had a great time. But I never once saw it as cheating on my wife's memory."

This surprises me. "Why not?"

"Because, kid, she's dead—and she'd want me to be happy. And if I went on ahead of her and she was stuck here, I'd want her to be happy too.

"I keep trying to tell you, Henry, it's not just that Cara's dead. It's good you grasped that part, but the flip side is, you're still alive. And if Cara knew you were trying to live like a goddamn monk to mourn her memory, and going half crazy with guilt when you find a nice girl, she'd probably smack some goddamn sense into you."

I think about it, and then have to laugh a little. "You're probably right. But it seems like it's kinda too late for your advice. Bethany's still not returning my calls."

He just smiles. "Give her time, kid. Seems like you've got some thinking to do about your life right now anyway."

I heave a sigh as I stare down the slope at my home. *Bethany.* "Well, you've got that part right."

Like the ancient house I live in, I'm a fixer. And I need to do most of that work myself.

CHAPTER TWELVE

Bethany

I spend three days in my apartment, avoiding everyone, not answering my phone. My heart feels like a stone in my chest, and I only remember to eat or sleep when I'm really in need.

Henry tries to call me a few times a day. He offers gentle, abject apologies and awkwardly asks if I will call him back so we can talk this out. He never calls before nine in the morning or after nine at night.

Michael calls me one hundred and thirty-six times on the one day he's out of jail, and fills up my voice-mail box with threats. I don't know where he gets all the burner phone numbers from, but he always has a new one when I block the last. He starts when he's released around dawn and doesn't stop until the police pick him up again.

Both of their messages make me cry for totally different reasons. Michael for the shame of ever having been with him. Henry for the disappointment, the anger, the fear that I will never truly be someone he loves...when I am already falling for him.

On the afternoon of the third day, Dr. Kaplan shows up at my door. I jump when I hear the knock, and shiver in fear of another Michael encounter until I hear her call out.

"Bethany," she says in a sharper voice than I am used to, "I'm going to have to insist that you let me in."

I push myself out of my chair and unlock the door. I barely have time to step aside before she comes sweeping in with full grocery bags in each arm. "Whoah—what is this?"

"You missed your appointment," she says cheerfully. "You never miss your appointment, not without calling. Given the new love in your life, and your ex throwing a literally flaming tantrum, I imagined you were down in the dumps."

I force a smile and go to fill up the kettle. "I didn't know you made house calls."

"I don't, normally. But normally my patients don't deal with people trying to burn down their homes." She sets the bags down beside my coffee table and starts unloading them onto it.

I stare at the assortment of fruits, veggies, pastry, breads, cheese, hummus and peanut butter, and then looked back up. "You know you're enabling my hiding indoors by bringing me food."

"I know that you'll hide indoors until your cupboards run dry to avoid any chance of running into Michael. But you need to eat—and fortunately for you, he won't be coming back around for a good long while." She winks and opens a bottle of sports drink, handing it to me.

"Sorry, what?" I blink at her blankly. I have been dreading the day Michael gets out of jail.

"Michael punched a cop on his way to having bail set last night. You won't be hearing from him for a bit."

I stare at her, then deflate and take a long swallow of the

drink. "Thank you for checking on that and telling me," I say hoarsely, grateful tears prickling my eyes. That leaves me with only one problematic man in my life to deal with.

"I thought it would do you some good to hear that," she says proudly. "Anyway, so tell me what happened with Henry."

I shudder and take a deep breath. "I think I may have just been a stand-in for him after all," I start.

"I'm listening."

It takes me twenty minutes to explain it all. Henry's fuckup and his making it worse with the way he handled it. My disappointment and sadness. My doubts, which caught fire when he once again called me by his lost wife's name.

"I don't know if he's so far gone he can't tell the difference, or if he's soothing himself in some way by pretending I'm her. But every time he calls me by her name I..."

"Wonder if it's really you he wants at all?" She finishes my sentence neatly, and I sigh and nod. "Oh honey.

"Look, the man's a trauma survivor. He's going to have some baggage. And there are some things that you shouldn't put up with. But the question I have for you is this: are they dealbreakers the moment that they happen, like cheating, or are they things you should not put up with twice?"

I have to really think about that. "He should have never called me by Cara's name, even if it was some kind of Freudian slip from trying too hard not to do it. And he should have never waited to tell me about a problem like the ripped condom."

"But he did these things. The question is, if he never does them again, is it worth giving him a second chance?" She chuckles. "I know being a better man than Michael isn't difficult, but even with his mistakes...Henry has been good for you, hasn't he?"

I think about that wild, wonderful weekend in his arms, and how happy I was when I came home. It's not just the contrast with Michael that makes Henry special, I realize. And I find myself nodding.

"Maybe you should think about taking another trip to the mountains once you've eaten and slept," she suggests gently.

Some conversations shouldn't be done over the phone. I know it, and so does my therapist. So I make the drive.

By the time that I make my way up the private road to the Castle, I'm nervous. I haven't answered any of Henry's phone calls, or given him any indication that I'm coming back. He gets even more depressed than I do.

Will he be all right?

A tall, older man who looks a little like Henry opens the door when I knock. He peers at me...and then smiles. "You Bethany?"

I feel a trickle of hope. "Yes. I'm here to see Henry, if he's around."

"Good. I'm Jake. Kinda been hoping you would show up." He jerks his head toward the side yard. "Take the path up the hill. He's saying goodbye to someone."

I find Henry back among the trees, standing inside a small family graveyard. He's laid roses on one of the gravestones within, and I can hear him talking quietly.

"Every time I see her face, I think of you. I guess it must look like I'm trying to replace you. But that's not it. I just feel guilty."

I pause, eyebrows rising. *What?*

"I spent twenty years alone because I didn't want to cheat on you. And here comes this hot, amazing woman who looks just like you, and every time I look at her face I'm reminded that I'm sleeping with someone who isn't you."

...Wait. So he's not delusional about who I am, he's feeling guilty for the reminder that he's sleeping with someone who isn't Cara? I'm not a substitute?

I'm...so much not her that he feels guilty about it?

Suddenly I'm glad to be lingering there listening. It's a bit dishonest, but...I needed to hear this.

"I don't know if reincarnation happens, or happened here, or if some other crazy thing is responsible. Or just coincidence. But Cara...I've mourned enough. I want to live."

Tears blur my vision as I watch him. My heart feels something sharp and icy fall from around it, and warms in my chest.

He sighs and shifts his weight before going on. His hands are shoved deep in his pockets. "I'm sorry I wasn't a better guy for you. I failed you, and now I've messed up again with Bethany.

"But Bethany's alive, Cara. I can try again. So once I'm done here, I'm going to Boston to try and fix things."

I swallow the lump in my throat and close my eyes on tears.

"You don't have to go to Boston to fix things," I say quietly.

He spins around, and his eyes widen. For a moment I worry he'll be angry—but when the relief breaks across his rugged face, my heart lifts, and I'm glad I came back here.

"I'm right here. And I'll stay as long as I'm needed."

"Bethany," he breathes. He crosses the ground in two strides, and hugs me fiercely enough that my feet almost leave the ground.

"That may be a long time," he whispers hoarsely into my hair.

I smile. "That's all right. These mountains are my home."

CHAPTER THIRTEEN

Bethany

"Real hot out there today," Henry says as he walks in with a colander of fresh-picked strawberries in his hands. "How's it going?"

I SIGH, glad again of the Castle's air-conditioned coolness. These days I'm especially susceptible to heat, which is why Henry's shooed me indoors while he does the gardening. But I've been wrestling with my own problems while he's been sweating in the heat.

"WELL, the book's coming together, but some of the information I gathered turned out to be a little disappointing." I gesture to the laptop on the desk in front of me. "Nothing from the genealogy folks showed any connection between Cara and I. There's no genetic explanation for why we're practically twins."

. . .

"Damn, that's bizarre." He's calm about it. After almost a year together, his attacks of grief over Cara are getting less and less frequent.

It's not just because I'm here for him now. He's realized that there can be no us until Cara becomes part of his past, and he no longer dwells on his worst memories of her.

That's exactly why I'm writing his memoir of their life together. It's a way of both honoring her whole memory, instead of just the memory of her death, and also putting those memories in a healthier context than constant self-torture. It's a labor of love for both of us.

It's also something to do while I can't move around so well.

"How's your back?" he asks gently as he looks over my shoulder at the family tree on the screen. Cara's and mine, side by side. They don't intersect.

We will never know, I suspect, why I bear such a strong resemblance to Cara, or how Henry and I managed to meet in the same violent, scary way that he lost her. All the other theories we can come up with—reincarnation, serendipity, Cupid giving us both a break—only sound plausible when I have enough wine in me, and I've had to stop drinking for a while.

"I could use a hot pad," I admit, giving him a wry smile. "The little poop's been kicking me for hours."

. . .

He helps me out of the chair, and it still takes an effort. I feel like I weigh about a million pounds. "Ungh, I can't believe I have to deal with another month of this."

"Hang in there, mama," he reassures, rubbing my back as I straighten and head for the kitchen. "It'll be worth it in the end. Now let's get these strawberries washed and onto some ice cream."

I smile and walk with him, ignoring my perpetual late-term pregnancy backache. Everybody's got problems they have to work through. Some linger for years, like scars, then fade. Others turn into something wonderful, with enough time and work.

Henry and I are veterans of both. And though the past may have broken us, the present is all about healing. And that will make for a better future together—for us and our child.

The End.

SIGN UP TO RECEIVE FREE BOOKS

Sign Up to Receive Free E-Books and Audiobook Codes.

Would you like to read **The Unexpected Nanny, Dirty Little Virgin** and **other romance books** for **free**?

You can sign up to receive these free e-books and audiobooks by typing this link into your browser:

https://www.steamyromance.info/free-books-and-audiobooks-hot-and-steamy/

Or this one:

https://www.steamyromance.info/the-unexpected-nanny-free/

PREVIEW OF SECRETS & DESIRES

A CHRISTMAS ROMANCE (SEASON OF DESIRE 1)

By Michelle Love

Blurb

Reclusive billionaire Nox Renaud has lived in New Orleans for most of his life, and at thirty-eight, he has been an enigma to the city's elite social circles ... except for once a year when he hosts a Halloween party at his sprawling mansion in the bayou, the one chance for the most beautiful women in Louisiana high society to get a glimpse at the handsome philanthropist. Nox has yet to fall in love or even date any of them—much to their chagrin. When grad student Livia Chatelaine is asked to waitress at the party, she jumps at the chance to earn some more money to help pay the rent on her tiny apartment in the French Quarter. Largely ignored by the rich partygoers, Livia works the party, but when she slips out into the grounds to get some air, she strikes up a conversation with the handsome young man she finds out there.

Not realizing he is her host, and therefore her employer for the night, Livia and the man talk. Their mutual attraction is obvious, but when they are interrupted by Amber Duplas—a lifelong friend of Nox's—Livia suddenly realizes who he is and, embarrassed, makes herself scarce.

She can't stop thinking about him, however, and when he seeks her out at her workplace and asks her out to dinner, they begin to date quietly. Their relationship quickly turns sexual, and despite their different circumstances, they begin to fall in love. Nox introduces her to a whole new world of hot, passionate sexual adventure. When Thanksgiving comes around, Nox even introduces her to the people he calls family at a fun and happy dinner.

Just when things are going so well, strange things start to happen. Livia starts getting threats at her college, and when dead bodies start turning up, Livia knows it won't be long before the killer comes after her. Nox's dark past is revealed, and Livia suddenly finds herself in a world of jealousy, obsession, and murder.

As Christmas draws near, Livia is terrified for her very life and wonders if she will end up as the next victim of the Renaud family curse …

CHAPTER ONE

Amber Duplas squinted at her oldest and dearest friend as he handed her a plate of perfectly-cooked eggs. "Nox Renaud, you are a pain in my ass."

Nox, his green eyes amused, grinned at her. "Well then, my work here is done. But why?"

Amber sighed and bunched her auburn hair up into a ponytail. "You're one of the wealthiest land owners in New Orleans, an incredibly successful businessman, *and*—according to Forbes—one of the world's most eligible bachelors. And yet you stand in your own palatial kitchen ..." she gestured around the vast room, "cooking me eggs for brunch *yourself*. Haven't you heard of chefs?"

Nox shook his head. He was used to this line of questioning from Amber. "You know I don't like a lot of people around me, Ambs."

Amber forked some egg into her mouth, almost swooning at the taste. "Which is why you're a pain. I'm worried that you'll become a hermit."

"I think hermithood arrived a while ago," Nox said mildly. "Look, I know you mean well, but I'm nearly forty, and I'm set in my ways. I like being alone." He dumped a panful of eggs onto his own plate and sat down. "And anyway, in a few days, the best and brightest will be here to drink my champagne and bother me all night. God, why do I do this every year?" He groaned and Amber laughed.

"Such a Grinch." She ruffled his dark curls and he grinned, though he was sighing on the inside. The Renaud family had given a Halloween charity benefit since way before Nox's birth—it had been a special project of his beloved mother's. Before the tragedy, of course. Despite his solitary nature, Nox could not bear to dishonor his mother's legacy.

His eyes flicked over to the framed picture of her and Teague, his adored elder brother, on the kitchen counter. Both of them dark and beautiful, laughing and hugging. Both of them gone so senselessly.

The tragedy of the Renaud family was known throughout Louisiana and beyond. Tynan Renaud, a respected businessman, adoring husband to the Italian-born Gabriella, and heroic father to his sons Teague and Nox, had suffered a psychotic break and gunned down his wife and eldest son one night before turning the gun on himself. Nox, away at college at the time, had been destroyed. After dropping out of school and coming home to the huge plantation mansion out on the Bayou, he had struggled for years to understand what his father had done.

Amber and his other friends had tried to persuade him to sell the place where his mother and brother had been murdered, but Nox refused. He took over his brother's business with his friend Sandor, and together, they had made a success of it. The company, RenCar, quickly became an outlet to forget his pain, with Nox pouring twenty hours a day into the work. Luxury food importing had never been his dream—was it anyone's?—but he had found something he was good at, and that was enough for him. His boyhood dreams of becoming a musician were pushed aside for something that would utterly distract him. The studio his mother had set aside for both of them to work in had stood empty for almost twenty years now ... as had Nox's heart.

He realized he wasn't listening to Amber now and apologized. She rolled her blue eyes. "Nox, I'm used to you spacing out on me, but listen, this is your party. I'm just saying, why don't you try to be more gregarious for a change? These people pay a lot of money to come here."

"Mostly to see the murder house," he mumbled, and Amber made an annoyed click with her tongue.

"Maybe so, but the money we raise goes to a good cause, doesn't it? Something good to come out of—damn it, Nox, you're not the only one who lost someone." To his horror, he saw tears in her eyes. He reached over and took her hand.

"Ambs, I'm sorry, I know. I miss Ariel too, every day." He sighed. *So much pain, so much death.* Amber was right; he needed to get out of this self-pitying funk.

"All I ask is for you to do your part on the night. Mingle and talk to your guests." Amber's tone was calmer now and she smiled at him, her face soft and her eyes on his, holding them for a beat too long. Nox nodded, looking away finally.

"I promise."

After Amber had gone, he wandered into his living room and flicked on the television. Local news station WDSU was doing a feature on Halloween New Orleans, the magical, manic mayhem of the festival the city threw every October. Nox sighed and waited for the inevitable mention of his party. "Wait for it," he muttered to himself. "Will it be the *Renaud Family Curse* or the *Mansion with the Dark Secrets*, first?"

The anchor looked serious. "Of course, before the festivities kick off on Halloween night, the New Orleans elite will gather at the Renaud mansion out on the Bayou. Regular viewers will know that the annual *Creepy Cocktails Gala Benefit* is held every year at the place some locals call 'the mansion with a dark history.' More on that after these messages."

Nox clicked off the television with an annoyed flick of his hand. Same story every year, and now his guests who watched the news would be all the more curious about the only remaining Renaud. *Damn it.*

His cellphone rang and he answered it gratefully. "Sandor, man, you have impeccable timing."

His friend laughed. "Any time. Listen, we may have a deal on the Laurent restaurant chain."

Nox sat up. "Really?" The Laurent business was worth twice what they had offered, but had been on the market for two years with no interest. Nox knew if they got it at a cheap price and refurbished it, it could make them a fortune. He and Sandor had decided to branch out into buying restaurants to serve their luxury foods as a new income stream—not that either of them needed it, but they both were bored with their business. They wanted to get their hands dirty and *do* something—something physical rather than just importing food for, well, people like them.

"Yep. Gustav Laurent is getting a divorce and he wants to get rid of the property quickly."

Nox was astonished. "*Gus* is divorcing *Kathryn?*"

"Seems so. Seems like she was sleeping around on him."

Nox made a half-amused, half-scornful noise. "Like Gustav hasn't been fucking around on her for years."

"You know Gus."

"Sadly, yes. Listen, I can be there in a half hour."

"Good," Sandor replied. "And, afterward, I'll spot you lunch. Deal?"

Nox smiled down the phone. "Deal. See you then."

. . .

Livia Chatelaine balanced three plates expertly along her left arm and carried them to the table. The two women and the child seated at the table smiled gratefully at her as she laid their food in front of them and returned their grins. "Enjoy, folks. Let me know if you need anything else."

She skirted back to another table that was waiting for their check and settled up with them quickly and with her innate friendliness. She had been working at Le Chat Noir café in the French Quarter for three months now, ever since she had packed her whole life into her battered old Gremlin and driven across the country from San Diego.

Moriko, her best friend from college, had been in New Orleans for a year and had gotten her the job at the café—it didn't hurt that the owner, a handsome, dark-haired Frenchman called Marcel, had a huge crush on Moriko and would have hired *anyone* she recommended. Thankfully, though, Livia and Marcel had become good friends, and Livia showed up early, stayed late, and worked her ass off for him. In return, he gave her the shifts that fit best with her studies and paid her enough that she could afford the tiny apartment she shared with Moriko.

Livia had decided as she left San Diego that she wouldn't return to her hometown again. It held no interest for her now, and there wasn't any family left there that she cared about. An only child, her mother had died when she was young, and Livia had brought herself up. She'd worked hard at school and at various jobs to put food on the table, while her father drank himself into a stupor every night and screamed at her if she disturbed him. Livia had stopped caring years ago about the man. As far as she was concerned, he was merely the sperm donor. What she remembered of her mother were warm, happy memories. Cancer was a fucker and it had stolen her happiness away when she was five. Livia's last memory of her mother was of the beautiful woman kissing her goodbye one day before school, and that was the last time she had seen her. Her father hadn't let her see her after she died.

Livia had put herself through college on a scholarship and by working three jobs, and it had become second nature to always fight and scrape for everything. It gave her energy and reason, and when she had graduated top of her class, it had all been worth it. Her tutors had been loath to let her go and had championed her to apply for post-graduate research scholarships, but it had taken Livia four years to finally secure an offer from the University of New Orleans.

"Hey, dreamer." Moriko nudged Livia out of her reverie and her friend smiled at her. Moriko, a tiny Japanese-American of exquisite beauty— and she knew it—hoisted herself up onto the counter. "Marcel needs a favor."

Livia hid a grin. When Marcel sent Moriko to do his dirty work it meant that, whatever the favor was, it would be a big— and probably inconvenient—one. "What is it?"

"Well, he's been asked to cater the Renaud party on Saturday. You know which one I mean?"

Livia shook her head. "Nope."

Moriko rolled her eyes. "It's an annual thing Nox Renaud does. He throws a Halloween gala party and gives a ton of money to charity."

"Never heard of him, or it. So, what's the favor?" Livia thought she could guess—Marcel needed waitstaff. A moment later, Moriko confirmed her suspicions.

"He was going to hire in silver service staff, but apparently they don't want anything but canapés and cocktails. Silver service staff would cost him more than he's making so ..."

Livia smiled at her. "It's no problem. Usual uniform?" She

pulled down on her too-tight white shirt and tucked it back into the black mini she wore to serve. It barely contained her lush curves—her full breasts and softly curved belly. Her legs, long and slender, were encased in black tights and she wore flat pumps, absolutely refusing to wear heels to wait tables. Livia wasn't the tallest girl, but her long legs made her look taller than her five-five height, and her long tawny waves were her crowning glory. She had pulled her almost waist-length hair into a bun, but it was forever escaping the clips. Moriko grabbed it now and twisted it up for her. Livia shot her a grateful smile. "Thanks, boo. I really should cut it all off."

"No way," Moriko said, her own shiny black hair falling in a straight curtain down her back. "I'd kill for your curls."

"So, Saturday night, waitressing for the rich muckety-mucks?"

"I'll be there too. Hey, at least we get to snoop around the rich guy's house."

Livia sighed to herself. She honestly didn't mind helping Marcel out, but she had very little time for rich boys with too much money. She'd had to wait on them enough in her time.

She went back out to the café and grimaced. Two regulars had just come into the restaurant. *Speaking of rich muckety-mucks,* she thought, plastering a fake smile on her face. The woman, an icy-looking blonde with bright red lipstick and cold blue eyes, looked at her dismissively. "Egg white omelet with spinach and a mangotini." She didn't look at the menu once. Her companion, a suave-looking man who at least smiled at Livia and said please and thank you whenever he was in, nodded.

"Same for me please, Liv. Good to see you again."

Livia smiled at him. She judged him for the company he kept, but if she was fair, he was always polite to her. She knew his companion was called Odelle, and her father was one of the richest men in the state. It didn't impress Livia. "You too, sir. Sure

I can't interest either of you in some French fries to go with your salad?"

Odelle looked horrified, but her companion grinned. "Why not?"

Livia grinned and disappeared into the kitchen. Marcel slunk in and smiled at her. "Thanks for Saturday, Livvy. I'll pay you double."

She kissed his cheek. "No problem, pal."

Marcel, his eyes so dark you couldn't see the pupils, nodded to the restaurant. "I see Elsa and Lumiere are in the restaurant."

Livia laughed. "You're getting your Disney all mixed up, and anyway, he's okay. But, yeah, she is the Ice Queen."

"Don't let their wealth get to you. It was all inherited, not earned."

"Oh, I know, and it doesn't bother me. Money can't buy breeding," Livia shrugged off the woman's rudeness. "I can honestly say these people and their ways don't keep me up at night, Marcel."

"I'm just saying because I know the man, Roan Saintmarc, is Nox Renaud's best friend. It's more than likely they'll be at the party on Saturday." Marcel grinned at Livia, who rolled her eyes. "Just promise me you won't tip their meals into their laps."

Livia snorted. "I promise, honey."

"Good girl."

Livia finished out her shift, then walked home through the busy streets of the French Quarter. She had fallen in love with this city—the slow, sensual heat, the sultry, laidback nature of the people. Strangely, for a city known for its voodoo and black magic, she had never felt uneasy walking the streets at night here.

Moriko was still at work when Livia got back to their apartment, so Livia took a long hot shower, then made herself a bowl of soup, grabbing some saltines from the pack in the kitchen. As she ate, she flicked through the television channels, but soon got bored. Dumping her bowl in the sink, she washed it out, then decided to go to bed to read. She had a piano recital coming up and she wanted to go through the score again, miming her key strokes in the air. She fell asleep with Moriko's cat cuddling in next to her and didn't hear her roommate come home.

OUT ON THE BAYOU, Nox too had fallen into a deep sleep, but his was not so peaceful. Almost instantly the nightmares came. A woman, a beautiful young woman he knew but one whose face he could not see, was calling to him, begging him to save her. There was blood, so much blood, and he ran through the darkened mansion, wading through something—blood?—to get to her. A dark, malevolent force overcame everything, stopping Nox from reaching the girl. He heard her screams cut off abruptly and knew he was too late. He sank to his knees.

He felt a hand on his shoulder and looked up. His mother was smiling at him. "Don't you know you'll never save them?" she said softly. "Everyone you love will die, my beloved son. I died, your father, your brother ... Ariel. You'll always be alone."

Nox awoke, gasping for air in a pool of his own sweat, the certainty of his dream mother's words screaming around his mind.

Don't fall in love. Don't risk it. Don't let anyone else get hurt.

CHAPTER TWO

Odelle Griffongy lit another cigarette and stood out on the balcony of her bedroom. She hated this holiday and hated this party. And yet Roan, of course, wanted to support his best friend, Nox, and so now they were getting dressed to attend. Thank *fuck* Nox never had a dress code for the cocktail party—Odelle would have feigned a headache otherwise.

She looked back into the bedroom where Roan was dressing, his dark gray suit spectacular with his coloring—medium brown hair and bright blue eyes. Ripped to the max, his hard body and his huge cock made him a machine in bed. Roan Saintmarc was, with the exception of Nox, the handsomest man in New Orleans—probably the state, even—and he was *hers*.

Odelle might have been brought up in the upper echelons of New Orleans society, but she knew her brittle beauty would only last so long and that her cool, aloof nature wouldn't make her many friends. That's why she was staggered when Roan, known as the fun-loving one in his group of Harvard grad friends, made a play for *her*. He could have had anyone.

Odelle turned back to see the crowds on the streets of the

city. New Orleans went crazy for Halloween—parties everywhere, people haunting the streets, and the locals playing up the myths and legends to sell more drink, food, and tourist crap. The normally serene street where Odelle and her cohorts lived were no different: pumpkins and jack o' lanterns, trees bedecked with twinkle lights and fake cobwebs, and Odelle's least favorite thing: kids trick or treating at every house.

Her doorbell rang, and although Odelle knew her staff would answer it, she couldn't help an irritated, "Oh, fuck off." Her voice carried down to the street, and she heard Roan's throaty laugh from behind her.

"Don't be a bitch, Delly. It's a rite of passage, trick or treating."

Odelle made a disgusted noise. "I never did that."

Roan smiled at her, sliding his arms around her waist. "No, you were too busy casting spells and mixing potions."

Odelle studied him coolly. "You think I'm a witch?"

"Cue cheesy line from me about you casting a spell on me. No, baby, I don't think you're a witch, and—mostly—not even a bitch. You just have a warmth deficiency." He said it with a grin, and although Odelle knew he meant it as a joke, it still stung.

Because it's true, she told herself. *What is wrong with me? Why can't I be more like Roan?* Or Nox, whose heart was so big it actually scared Odelle. Or even Amber, her frenemy, who had once had a thing with Roan. *No*, Odelle told herself. *Don't go there. Not tonight.* She attempted a smile as Roan brushed his lips against hers.

"You're right. It's just one night."

"That's my girl." Roan looked her up and down in her tight black dress and when his gaze met hers, Odelle saw the desire in his eyes. "Nox won't mind if we're a little late."

Odelle smiled and, turning, she bent over the balcony and hitched her skirt up to her waist. She heard Roan chuckle.

"Out here? What *will* the neighbors think?" But then, with a grunt, she felt him thrust into her from behind, his massive cock reaming her cunt as he gripped the metal balustrade with both hands.

Odelle closed her eyes, reveling in the feeling of him filling her so completely. Her hand drifted down to stroke her clit as he fucked her, and soon she was moaning and shivering through one orgasm after another, not caring who heard her. Roan was a brutal lover, especially when he came, and Odelle winced as he thrust harder and harder until he blew his load inside of her and withdrew, panting for air and cursing softly with release. He spun her around and ground his mouth down on hers. "God, woman, you drive me fucking crazy."

Odelle smiled and squeezed his diminishing cock in her hands. "Do that to me once more and then we can go to the party."

And they began again.

Livia and Moriko helped Marcel and his sous-chef Caterina—Cat—load the trays of canapés into the restaurant's van before Liv and Moriko hopped in the back for the drive to the Renaud Mansion. Livia was trying to keep the trays from tipping and tying her thick mane up into a chignon at the same time, but the weight of it would not stay clipped. Moriko grinned at her.

"Just pull it back. You'll never get it all up."

"I refuse to be beaten," Livia muttered. Eventually, Moriko pushed Livia's hands out of the way.

"Let me."

As Livia held the trays of food, Moriko deftly worked Liv's hair into a messy bun at the nape of her neck. "That's the best you're going to get, girl, so live with it."

Livia tentatively patted it. "You're a miracle worker. From now on, I'll pay you to be my hair wrangler."

Moriko laughed. "You couldn't afford me."

When they arrived at the mansion, they were stunned into silence. The old plantation home had been modernized to some extent—a plaque on the door detailed its history and its passage to the Renaud family in the 1800s, wherein all slaves were freed and the plantation became a family homestead rather than a working freehold.

The imposing white building with shuttered windows and soft light radiating from within was decorated with high-quality Halloween trimmings. Moriko grinned at Livia as they passed a batch of expertly carved pumpkins. "You think they got Michelangelo to do them?"

Livia rolled her eyes. The place screamed money and opulence, but Livia wasn't impressed. As they moved into the kitchen, she saw Marcel talking to a young man who was dressed in a dark navy sweater and jeans, and who Livia guessed was the owner's assistant. He had dark curls and the most intense—and beautiful—green eyes she had ever seen.

The stranger sensed her scrutiny and looked up. Their eyes met and Livia felt a shudder of desire ripple through her. God, if even the *staff* looked like supermodels here …

She nudged Moriko. "Does Marcel want us to change now or after we've set up?"

"After. Apparently, there's a dedicated room for us."

"Fancy."

"I know, right? Usually we have to squat in the back of the van to get ready."

Livia snorted and, between them, they quickly arranged the canapés on the silver trays. When they had finished, Livia saw the handsome assistant had gone and Marcel was nodding at them. "Lovely job. The food looks great. So, this thing kicks off in an hour, but guests are starting to arrive, so we'll start with the welcome pumpkin-spice sidecars first up. Think you can cope?"

"No worries, boss," Moriko hugged Marcel, who turned red with pleasure. "We'll show these rich kids a good time ... wait, that sounded dirtier than I meant it to."

Livia snorted with laughter as Moriko shrugged. "Come on then. Let's get dressed."

A HALF HOUR LATER, Livia was regretting the tightness of her skirt. It had been her go-to throughout college—short, black, and figure-hugging even back then when she was ten pounds lighter. She'd dragged it out of her closet this morning—it had been the cleanest, most professional skirt she could find. *I need to go shopping,* she told herself as she plastered a smile on her face and made the rounds with a tray of drinks.

The mansion's main ballroom ("*Main* ballroom," she'd muttered to an amused Moriko. "Because the other ballrooms are too *small*.") was decorated beautifully, even the cynical Livia had to admit. Twinkle lights draped the walls and soft music was playing as the guests milled around, talked, and drank. Moriko was making the first pass with a canapé tray, and Livia could tell her friend was gritting her teeth, fending off unwanted remarks and come-ons.

"Hey, Livvy." She heard Roan Saintmarc's voice behind her and turned. She was actually relieved to see a friendly face; if the guests weren't turning their noses up at her presence or trying to talk her into bed, they looked through her as if she were invisible. Roan's smile was friendly. He indicated the man he was talking with, a tall, dark-haired man with a neatly-trimmed beard and dark brown eyes.

"San, this is my friend from my favorite restaurant. Livia, this is Sandor Carpentier, a good friend of mine."

Sandor Carpentier had a warm, open smile as he shook Livia's hand. She grinned at them both, happy to see friendly faces at last. "Can I get you fellas a refill?" She waved the bottle of Krug she was holding and topped up their glasses. "Boss tells me the good bourbon will be out soon," she said with a wink.

"If I know Nox, it will be," Roan said, and looked around. "Speaking of whom, have you met our lord and master yet, Liv?"

She shook her head. "But he would probably tell me to get back to work. Nice seeing you, Mr. Saintmarc, Mr. Carpentier."

"Sandor, please," the man said, and Livia decided she liked his merry, twinkling eyes. He didn't seem as aloof as the others. "And if you knew Nox, you'd know that's unlikely. He'd probably insist you join us for a drink."

Livia smiled and made her excuses. Despite what they said, she didn't want Marcel to get into trouble if she was caught fraternizing with the guests. She made her way back to the kitchen to refill her tray. Moriko was just coming in from the garden.

"Hey, boo, I just finished up my break, and Marcel told me to let you grab one now that I'm done. There are a couple of good places to hide and take your shoes off out there."

Livia smiled at her friend gratefully and headed out of the kitchen door into the lush gardens. It was darker down here than at the front of the mansion, and she could see a fog coming in off the bayou at the end of the property. Livia thought it was much spookier, befitting the Halloween vibe of the party, and yet more beautiful than any of the decorations inside.

With a soft moan, she eased off her heels and wondered why she hadn't worn her usual flats. No, she knew why—she had wanted to make a good impression for Marcel. She knew she could pull off the cool professional vibe with her heels on, and at least it gave her a few extra inches when she needed to be seen. Still, her feet pulsed with pain, and when she put her hot soles on cool ground, she sighed with relief.

She crept barefoot into a little grove, and seeing the edge of a stone seat, headed for it. She stopped, seeing the other end was already occupied. "Sorry," she said, then saw it was the assistant she'd shared a moment with earlier.

He had changed out of his sweater and jeans and was now wearing what looked to be a very expensive black suit. *Perks of the job*, she suspected, but her attention was drawn by the way it fit his broad shoulders and slim figure so well. She meant to turn and go, but the sheer sadness in his eyes took her breath away. "Are you okay?" Her voice was soft, and the man stared at her, his eyes intense, before he half nodded, then shook his head.

"Not really, but common manners dictate I say I am. So ..." His voice was deep—a beautiful deep baritone that sent a shiver through her. Livia hesitated for a moment, then sat down next to him.

"Escaping from the melee? Me too. Just for a minute." She smiled at him, noticing again how gorgeous he was, except for that pain in his eyes. She wished she could take it away for him. "Are you hiding from the muckety-mucks?"

His mouth hitched up in a half-smile. "Kind of."

She leaned forward conspiratorially. "I won't tell," she whispered, and he laughed. It changed his whole face, turning it from brooding and slightly dangerous into a boyish, joyful thing.

"Right back at you." He looked at her name tag. "Livia. Not O-livia?"

She shook her head. "No, just Livia." She shivered at the cool air coming up from the water. "It really is beautiful here."

He nodded, and seeing her trembling, he shrugged out of his jacket and put it around her shoulders. She felt her face get hot. "Thank you."

They gazed at each other for a long moment, and Livia felt tongue tied. He smelled wonderful too, all clean linen and woodsy spice, and for a moment she found herself having to resist the urge to run her fingertips over his long, thick lashes. They were so black, they looked like he had eyeliner on.

She swallowed hard, the desire to kiss this stranger overwhelming and bewildering. She cast around for something to say. "I was thinking, that mist from the bayou must have known there was a Halloween party here tonight." *God, could she have sounded any dumber?* She cursed herself, but he smiled at her.

"I guess it must have known. I find it … romantic. Dark and malevolent, perhaps. But also sensual."

Livia could feel a pulse beating furiously between her legs and was amazed. She hadn't had this reaction to a man in forever … or *ever*, if she was being honest. Electricity hung in the air between them. She had to dispel it before she did something reckless. She had Marcel and Moriko to think about here.

She nudged him with her shoulder. "Hey, you better get in there before all the food is gone. Honestly, they're like sharks, these people. Fins and everything. The food is really good, too. I hope your boss agrees."

Another smile, amused and sweet. "I'm sure he does." He stood and offered his hand. "Shall we sneak into the kitchen and grab something, then?"

Trembling, she took his hand—the skin surprisingly soft and dry—and stood. "Okay. But afterward, you have to tell me your name."

Their bodies were really close now, and Livia could feel his body heat through her clothes. He trailed a finger across her cheekbone, and Livia shivered. She smiled, but stepped away from him. "I think we'd better get inside." *As much as I'd like to fuck you right here, right now.*

His smile didn't change and he squeezed her hand. "Of course."

"Nox!" They both heard the female's voice from across the garden. "Nox, where the hell are you?"

A thrill of panic went through Livia as her companion called out. "Right here, Ambs. Keep your shirt on."

I should have known ...

Livia was frozen. *Shit, shit, shit.* This was *Nox Renaud*. He smiled down at her and put his finger over his lips for a second before his smile widened into a conspiratorial grin. "I have to go."

She nodded and shrugged out of his jacket. "Here, you better have this back. I'm going inside now, anyway."

He thanked her, taking the coat, and with a last regretful look towards her, disappeared back towards the direction of the shouting woman.

"Oh fuck," Livia hissed to herself. "Way to be unprofessional. Catering one-oh-one, don't almost *kiss* the client. *Jesus.*"

Her face flaming with embarrassment, she went back into the kitchen and managed to work the rest of the party while avoiding any contact with Nox Renaud or his friends ... difficult, but not impossible. When it became clear the party was winding down, Livia hid out in the kitchen and dealt with the clean-up.

Marcel was all smiles when he came to thank them both. "Liv, you didn't need to do this," he said, looking in amazement at the stack of empty, clean trays she was loading into the van. She grinned at him.

"No problem, boss." She made herself busy untying her apron. "Did you get good feedback?"

"*Very* good feedback. And a somewhat unexpected bonus, which you'll find in your paychecks. No, don't argue. Say what you want about the Renaud family, but Nox is a very generous man. He also told me that I was his go-to caterer for the future, which isn't saying a lot because he rarely entertains guests, but it's still something."

"It *is* something. It's a *big* something." Moriko kissed Marcel's cheek and he gave her a hug.

"Thanks, Morry. He also said he'd be recommending me to his friends and clients. Good guy. Jeez, look at the time. Come on, kids, let's get out of here. I'll buy you both a late dinner."

LATER, at home in bed, Livia could not help but look up Nox Renaud on the internet. She flicked through pages of photos of him, drinking in the shape of his face, the green eyes that looked just as sad in his childhood pictures as in every photo of him as an adult. She traced his face with her finger. In some pictures he had a beard, which made him look even more handsome, she thought. When she began to read about his history—the murder/suicide of his parents and brother, the mysterious death of his teenage sweetheart, the years of suspicion aimed at Nox himself—she learned he'd been thoroughly investigated after the death of Ariel Duplas. Nox was only eighteen at the time and was the only suspect, but the police had completely exonerated him. The piece Livia was reading made it clear that his family's deaths had broken the handsome young man.

SINCE HIS FAMILY tragedy and the subsequent investigation, Renaud has kept a low profile. His luxury food importing business with friend Sandor Carpentier has made him a billionaire, but this has just served to draw more attention and comparisons to other tragic figures. Many locals refer to him as New Orlean's own Howard Hughes—a reclusive man with a myriad of secrets. Only once a year do we really get to see the man, at his annual benefit on Halloween, but it doesn't stop gossip magazines the world over wondering about the romantic life of this devastatingly—and some say, dangerously—handsome young man. As he approaches forty, will Nox Renaud ever break free of his past?

God, I hope so. The thought came unbidden to Livia as she slid her finger over his photograph. Not that it would have anything to do with her, but she had sensed something special in the man she had met—that he was more than just another handsome rich boy. There were hidden depths there, she was sure of it.

When she went to sleep that night, she dreamed of Nox Renaud and his beautiful green eyes, and of the moment his lips would press against hers.

CHAPTER THREE

Amber rolled her eyes as Nox sat down at the table. It was the French Quarter, with busy streets and lunchtime crowds, and the restaurant Amber had chosen was almost full. "You're late again, Renaud. Where's the Rolex I bought you last year?"

Nox sighed, kissing her cheek. "You know I don't like to wear it out in public. It looks too ostentatious. Not that I'm not grateful for it," he added, seeing Amber's frown, "it was a lovely gift. I just don't know if it's really *me*."

Amber opened her mouth to argue, then gave up. Nox looked different and had seemed different—lighter—since the party. Amber had wondered if it was just the relief of getting it over and done with for another year, but it had been a week since the party and every time she had seen him, Nox had been *happy*.

"What's going on with you?" she asked him now, and Nox, who was reading the menu, glanced up and smiled at her.

"What do you mean?"

"I mean ... you look different. You look ... lighter."

"I haven't lost weight, far from it."

Amber rolled her eyes again. Nox was nowhere in the vicinity of overweight. "I mean *emotionally*. You seem to be carrying yourself more cheerfully than usual."

Nox laughed, his green eyes twinkling. "Do I?"

"Fine, don't tell me then." Amber snatched the menu from him grumpily and sulked behind it. Nox smothered a grin.

"Ambs ... you ever have one of those moments in life, however fleeting, where someone or something just reminds you why you're alive? Someone who sets off a thought process that makes you reevaluate your entire existence?"

"Is this your fancy way of saying you got laid?" Amber felt a twinge of jealousy go through her and brushed it away. *He doesn't belong to you ... he never did.*

Nox shook his head. "No, I haven't ... no. I just had a moment with someone, a woman, at the party. I'd like to see her again, is all."

"Really?" Amber ran through all of the party guests in her head, and Nox just smiled and shook his head. "Who?"

Nox hesitated and smiled ruefully at her. "Can I just have this secret for a little bit? I swear, the moment it becomes more than a ... *moment* ... you'll be the first to know."

Amber relaxed. "Of course, honey." She reached over and squeezed his hand. "I'm very happy for you. It's about time you got your pickle tickled."

Nox burst out laughing and Amber joined in, her blue eyes amused. As they ordered their food, she studied her friend. They had known each other for more than half their lives. They'd been drawn together by Amber's twin, Ariel, who had come home from school one day and told her family that she had met the most beautiful boy in the world.

She hadn't been wrong. Nox Renaud was the kind of boy that sculptors made statues of. That strong jaw, those perfectly symmetrical features. Big green eyes. Sensual mouth. *God.* More than once since Ariel's death, Amber had wondered if she and Nox would end up together—mostly out of convenience—but he'd never made an advance and she had never found the courage.

She had to admit, it hurt a little that Nox had finally shown interest in someone and it wasn't *her*, but she could not begrudge her friend his happiness. Amber's own love life was ... complicated. She always kept two lovers at a time, but never let either near her heart. Her beauty, her wealth, her position in society—she didn't need a husband, which made her lethal to the women of New Orleans, who kept their husbands away from her. Little did they know, Amber wasn't interested in any of them. What she wanted was far more complex. *Far more Nox-like,* she told herself, then pushed the thought away. He would never be hers, and she would have to accept that.

"So, when are you going to make your move?" she asked Nox, who blinked with nervousness. To her amazement, two spots of pink appeared on Nox's cheeks as he shrugged.

"I don't know. I've been working on getting the courage up to approach her."

Amber almost spat her water out. Nox Renaud—billionaire, drop-dead-gorgeous businessman—was *nervous* about asking a girl on a date. "Wow. I haven't seen you like this since ..."

She trailed off and looked away. Ariel was always there, always between them. Amber swallowed the lump in her throat. Nox's smile had faded and he nodded. "I *never* thought this day would come, Ambs ... and look, no one, *no one* will ever replace her."

"I know that, sweetie, but hopefully someone will mean just as much to you some day."

His eyes danced in a way she hadn't seen for years. "I hope so too, Ambs. I really hope so too."

. . .

Livia tried to stop thinking about Nox Renaud as she practiced her scales up and down, using the plain rhythm to distract herself. In the week since she'd met him, her body had felt wired, her brain whirling. To have that much chemistry with someone she probably would never see again … it didn't seem right. She faltered in her playing and then crashed her fingers down on the keyboard.

"Unless you're going for some kind of weird Stockhausen thing," a voice behind her said, "I'm guessing you're having an off day."

Livia turned to smile at her tutor. In the few months she had been at the college, her tutor, Charvi Sood, had become more than just a teacher to her. The two women had bonded over their love of jazz, of Monk, Parker, Davis, and to Charvi's delight, their mutual admiration for Judy Carmichael, the reason Livia had fallen in love with the genre. Listening to Carmichael's radio shows when she was living at home with her father, her headphones plugged in to dull the sound of her father shouting drunkenly at the television, she had used the genre as her way to transport herself out of the San Diego heat and here to New Orleans.

Charvi put down the stack of scores she had in her hand and peered over her glasses at her young student. "You okay? You've been in here practicing all week. You *can* rest, you know. It may be your master's degree, but rest is vital for brainpower."

Livia smiled at her. "I know. I'm trying to distract myself from thinking about a boy. It's very annoying."

Charvi laughed, shaking her head. "It happens to the best of us. Want to share?"

Livia picked out a tune with her forefinger. "It's embarrassing. He's way out of my league and—"

"Let me stop you there, young lady. *No one* is out of your league."

Livia sighed. "It's Nox Renaud."

That stopped Charvi. "Ah. Well, I would say the problem there isn't that you're out of his league, it's that he's Nox Renaud."

Livia looked at her friend curiously. "You know him?"

"I knew his mother. I've met Nox a few times. He's ... an enigma. At least if you believe the gossip."

"He has the saddest eyes I've ever seen, and he seemed so sweet. Lonely, but sweet. Nice. God, nice is such a bland thing to say, but he was friendly and warm and ..."

"You have an enormous crush on him."

Livia shrugged. "Yes, but it doesn't matter. It's not like we run in the same circles. Forget I said anything."

Charvi smiled. "Well now, let's channel that desire into your playing. Give me something slow and sensual. And make it up as you go along. Think about Mr. Renaud and let your fingers move across the keyboard."

At first Livia was embarrassed, feeling exposed, but as her fingers stroked the keys she began to find a melody. She closed her eyes and thought about the feeling of him trailing his finger across her cheek, the scent of his skin, the ocean-green color of his eyes. She played a melody so sweet she wanted to cry, and when she finished and opened her eyes, she felt her face burn red.

"Wow, you have it bad," Charvi teased her and held up her phone. "It needs work, but there's something there. I've recorded it and I'll email it to you. Your homework is to score it and mold it into a piece you can perform at the end of semester recital."

Livia gaped at her. "Are you kidding me?" She felt panicky at revealing something so personal to an audience. But Charvi nodded.

"I'm deadly serious. That was the most connected I've ever seen you with your piano, Liv." She checked her watch. "And I have a seminar. Work on it, Liv, and I swear you'll see what I mean."

Left alone, Livia checked her laptop. Charvi had indeed emailed her the MP3 and as Liv played it back, she realized there *was* something there. She grabbed some blank score paper and began to write.

NOX LOOKED up as Sandor knocked on the door jamb. "Hey."

Sandor grinned. "You still working? Dude, it's Friday night. Let's go out and have drinks."

Nox chuckled. "I would, but I'm waiting on a call from Italy. Haven't you got a date?"

Sandor shrugged. "She blew me off. I'm kind of relieved, to be honest. I'm getting too old to be dating a different pretty girl each week."

"My heart bleeds for you. So, I'm your consolation prize?"

Sandor grinned. "Yup. Grab your cell phone and take the call on that. We're going drinking."

Nox hesitated. "All right, but let's go to the French Quarter."

"Wanna mix with the tourists? Come on then."

AN HOUR and two shots of bourbon later, Nox relaxed back into his seat and glanced around the bar. He hadn't told Sandor that the bar he'd chosen was across the street from Marcel Pessou's restaurant—or that ever since they'd gotten here, Nox had been looking for any sign of Livia. He hadn't had one night of peace since he'd met her.

The feel of her soft skin, her huge chocolate brown eyes, the way her tawny hair fell in messy waves over her shoulders; it all haunted him. The faint flush of pink when he'd touched her face. He'd been so close to kissing her—which would have been *entirely* inappropriate. But, God, the feelings he had thought he'd never feel again were whirling and thrashing through him like a storm.

He had to see her again—to see if the connection between them hadn't been just *that* moment in time. To see if it was real, tangible, and something they could build on. Also he really, *really* needed to kiss her gorgeous pink mouth—it was driving him crazy.

"Nox? Buddy?"

Nox blinked back into the present. "Sorry, what?"

"I was saying, I was talking to Roan at the party. He seems pretty keen on working with us on the Feldman project."

Nox snorted and sipped his bourbon. "What does *Roan* know about the luxury food trade?"

"Nothing, but he does know about the *shipping* trade," Sandor gave Nox a reproachful look. "Look, I know you think he's a playboy, but he's got a good head on his shoulders. Besides … he wants to buy his way in."

"What?"

"He told me he wants us three to go into business together. He wants in on the company."

For the first time that night, Nox stopped thinking about Livia, leaning forward to study his friend. "How come he hasn't said anything to me?"

Sandor chuckled. "Because he *knows* you think he's a playboy. He's your best friend, but there's always been the joker in the pack, and it's always been Roan. He was feeling me out in the hope I'd do the approach. So, I am. I think it's something we should talk about. He wants to impress you, buddy, is all."

Nox considered. "I'm open to talking about it, certainly."

Sandor smiled. "So, I can tell him yes?"

"*Talking* about it, San. Nothing more at this stage."

"I love it when you get masterful. Another drink?"

"Go for it."

Nox leaned back, his eyes flicking automatically to the restaurant on the other side of the street. He could see the pretty Asian girl who was working with Livia at his party waiting on tables, but there was no sign of Livia. He thought about what Sandor had said. Roan was Nox's oldest friend but he was also someone who acted on impulse—he would best be described as reckless. Nox had worked too hard on the business, and not even his love for his friend could override the fact that Roan was not a good bet. Nox rubbed his eyes. Maybe he should loosen up, take a risk.

Take a risk ... His mind went back to the lovely girl he'd met at his party. Yes, he would take a risk. Enough of skulking like a creep across the street. Tomorrow, he would go the restaurant and ask for her. If she wasn't there, *he'd* leave his number. If she *was* there ...

He was still smiling when Sandor returned with the drinks.

IT WAS after midnight when Livia left the practice rooms, and as she didn't have enough cash on her for a cab, she decided to walk home. When she got back to the French Quarter, she decided to go the restaurant and see if Moriko wanted company on her walk home.

As she turned into an alley leading to Bourbon Street, she suddenly felt herself being jerked back, and a heavy arm locked around her throat. Shocked into action, she threw her elbows back with all her strength, cussing and screaming at her attacker. *"Get off me, motherfucker!"* She slammed her fist back into the man's groin and he groaned, releasing her.

Her anger at full flood and the adrenaline spiking in her system, Livia punched and kicked the mugger until, still groaning, he took off. Yelling *"Bitch!"* at her as he ran, she unleashed a litany of curse words at him, beyond caring who heard her. Finally, she caught her breath and picked up her bag, turning to go to the restaurant.

She stopped. Nox Renaud was looking at her, astonished admiration in his eyes. Livia's breath caught in her throat.

"Well," he said finally, a grin slowly spreading across his face. "Hello again."

CHAPTER FOUR

"I'm absolutely *fine*," Livia complained as Marcel fussed over her, making her drink the bourbon he offered. Nox Renaud sat across from her, a small smile playing around his lips. It was as if they shared a secret now, and Livia couldn't help but grin.

"I heard you holler," Nox told her, "and came to help, but you'd pretty much wrecked the guy by the time I got there. Pretty badass, if you ask me."

"A girl's got to look after herself," Livia said. She couldn't stop looking at him—she *hadn't* imagined how gorgeous he was. Those green eyes, that dark hair and messy curls, they were all as beautiful as she remembered. The way he was looking at her sent thrills through her entire body.

Marcel and Moriko seemed to notice the charged atmosphere and, after making sure Livia really was okay after the shock of her mugging, they discreetly disappeared. The restaurant was closed now, only a couple of lamps still on, and in the gloom, Nox took her hands in his.

"I haven't been able to stop thinking about you," he said honestly. "I admit, my friend and I came to the Quarter for drinks and I deliberately chose the bar across the street from here ... I hoped to see you."

"Which friend?"

"Sandor? You might have met him at the party."

Livia nodded. "I did. He seemed lovely."

Nox smiled. "He is. But as lovely as he is, I don't want to talk about Sandor. Liv, those few moments we spent together in the garden ... I don't want to presume, but to me, there was something there."

"I felt it too." She began to tremble as he got out of his seat and stepped closer to her. He was so tall, she felt tiny next to him. He pulled her out of her chair and slid his hands onto her waist—tentative, a question in his eyes.

"Is this okay?"

Livia nodded and Nox smiled. He bent his head and Livia felt —at last—his lips against hers. The first kiss was brief, hesitant. But it didn't stop at one, and went on, becoming more passionate, his fingers tangling in her long hair, pulling her closer. Livia could feel his heart beating in his chest as her own arms snaked around him, her hands feeling the taut muscles of his back.

Kissing him was like taking a shot of pure heroin, she imagined. Heady, overwhelming, electric. His lips shaped themselves perfectly to hers, his tongue caressing, massaging hers, his breathing ragged. Finally, desperate for air, they broke apart.

"Wow." Livia breathed. "*Wow.*"

Nox brushed his fingertips across her face. "Livia, may I please take you on a date?"

His words seemed so formal after that breathtaking kiss that she giggled. Nox grinned. "I'm sorry, I'm out of practice. What I mean is, I would like to see you again. And again. And *again*."

His words made her melt, and she leaned into his embrace. She gazed up at him. "I would like that too, Nox, very much. But

... what will your family, your friends think? I'm just a waitress. Well, a grad student, but I'm clearly not of your social circle. Won't they think badly of me?"

"I really don't care. There is no 'just' a waitress or a student. Both of those things are honorable, genuine things. But who cares what our jobs are? You're Livia, I'm Nox. The rest is just window dressing."

Livia gave a soft moan of desire and he tightened his arms around her. "I'd just like to get to know you, Liv. We can work anything else out together. Let's just try, that's all I ask."

HE WALKED her back to her apartment, but didn't ask to come in. He kissed her again and it was just as spine-tingling as their earlier kiss. She could feel the tension in his body, the way his huge erection pressed against her belly when he held her tightly, but Nox Renaud was clearly a gentleman. "May I see you tomorrow?"

So proper, so polite. She nodded, grinning. "Tomorrow is my day off, so yes."

"Then would you spend the day with me?"

"I'd like that very much."

Nox brushed his lips against hers, his hands gently cradling her face. "Then shall we say ten a.m.?"

"Perfect."

The kiss deepened, once again leaving Livia breathless. Nox smiled at her. "Goodnight, lovely Liv."

"Goodnight, Nox."

SHE FELT bereft as she saw him walk away, turning to look at her once more before he turned the corner. His grin made her heart swell. For a moment or two, she stood out in the cool night, blinking. "Did that actually just happen?"

She chuckled and went inside. As she opened the door to the apartment, Moriko, dressed in Hello Kitty pajamas, held up a bag of potato chips and said, "You, on the couch, *now*. You're not going to bed until you've told me *everything*."

HE HAD WATCHED Nox and the girl, Livia, walk back to her apartment, following at a safe distance. They were obviously smitten with each other, and he guessed they must have met at the party. The party where she was a *waitress*, and Nox was the billionaire party host. He couldn't fault Nox on his taste. Livia was beautiful, all sumptuous curves and softness. But still, a waitress ... The scandal would be great indeed, especially amongst their cohorts, but that wasn't what was making him smile. No, it was the thought of Nox and Livia possibly falling deeply in love, so deeply in love that when she was taken from him, Nox would finally be destroyed.

And that was all he had ever dreamed of ...

CHAPTER FIVE

Moriko was sitting on the bathroom cabinet, watching Livia apply her makeup. "I cannot believe you didn't sleep with him."

Livia rolled her eyes. "Dude, we haven't even been on a date yet."

"Prude."

Livia grinned. Moriko was a seize-the-moment kind of girl; Livia preferred the slow-burn. "Besides, if we'd had sex in the restaurant, Health and Human Services would have been outraged." God, just thinking about sex with Nox was making her hot, but she brushed the thought aside before Moriko could pick up on it. "Look, we're going on *one* date. Don't jump the gun."

"Where's he taking you?"

Livia sighed. "*We're* taking *each other* ... I don't know. We haven't discussed that yet."

"Too busy sucking face."

Livia laughed aloud. "Well, do you blame me? Have you seen him? Now, go away, I need to finish up here and you're distracting me."

Moriko hopped down, grinning, and tapped a closed drawer. "Plenty of condoms in there. Take a handful. Better safe than sorry."

Livia pointed out at the door and, grumbling but grinning, Moriko left her alone. Livia shut the door behind her and sighed, leaning against it. Her whole body felt as if she were wired up to the National Grid. If Nox even touched her once, she would jump him. "Calm the fuck down," she muttered to herself. Still, when she'd finished getting ready, she grabbed some condoms from the drawer and shoved them deep into her purse.

Nox was five minutes early. "Sorry, couldn't wait."

Livia saw Moriko make a crude gesture behind Nox's back and glared at her. "Do excuse Moriko; she was raised by wolves."

"All the best people are," Nox grinned at Livia's friend, who smiled back at him.

"Look after her," she said. "Later, lovers." She disappeared back into her bedroom while Livia's face burned red.

"So," she said, trying not to look flustered in his presence, "what's the plan?"

"Well, last night your roommate told me you hadn't been in New Orleans for long, so I thought maybe we could take a steamboat trip. We could see the city and talk at the same time. What do you think?"

Livia smiled at him. "I think that sounds perfect."

THE STEAMBOAT NATCHEZ was full of tourists as it began to float down the Mississippi River, but neither Nox nor Livia cared. They sat out on the deck, the weather still very warm despite it being November, breathing in the fresh air. Nox asked Livia about where she had come from.

"Southern California, so I'm used to hot weather," she

grinned. "It is different heat here, more humidity. Sultrier. New Orleans is a very sexy city."

Nox laughed. "If you say so. I'm NOLA born and bred, but I have to admit, sometimes the heat during the day gets to me. So why did you leave SoCal?"

Livia looked away from his gaze. "No family to speak of, and Moriko was here. I managed to get a scholarship to the University, so that made it official. I haven't regretted it once. Especially now."

They smiled at each other and Nox leaned in to kiss her again. "Livia, that night at the party ... I haven't felt a connection like that in years."

"Really?" She was delighted, then frowned. "No, I mean, really? Look at you, you could have anyone."

"I'm fussy," he said lightly with a grin, but she could see something behind his eyes.

"You don't give away a lot, do you? I mean, I could see the sadness in your eyes when we met ... You can talk to me, you know?"

Nox's expression changed for a split second—fear?—but he shook his head. "I'm a firm believer in the past staying in the past. What I want now is for us to get to know each other. Is that something you'd like, Livvy?"

She studied him, leaning on the railing of the steamboat. "Charvi was right about you. You *are* an enigma."

"Charvi? Charvi Sood?" Nox's eyes lit up and Livia nodded.

"Yes, she knew your mother?"

"I'll say. Charvi was my mom's best friend." He looked so excited, like a little boy. "I had no idea she was back in New Orleans."

"She is. She's my tutor, my mentor, really. I'm sure she'd love to see you."

Nox gave a short laugh. "Why wouldn't she come to see me

herself?" He frowned to himself, obviously deep in thought, and Livia wondered if she had made a mistake mentioning Charvi to him.

Nox shook himself. "Well, yes, I'd love to see her." He smiled at Livia. "So, you're a master pianist?"

She laughed. "Oh, no, I'm really just a beginner, at least when you consider the scope of the craft. My focus is on jazz piano, for this program at least. But, really, I love all classical music. And rock, and blues, and on and on ..."

"I'm afraid my music knowledge extends as far as Pearl Jam and Tom Petty. That kind of music."

"I adore *both*," Livia encouraged him. "For my undergraduate thesis, for the recital, I did a slowed down piano version of "Rearviewmirror.""

"I gather speed, from you fucking with me ..." Nox quoted and their gazes locked. Livia felt breathless.

"Anticipation is a marvelous thing," she said softly and Nox nodded.

"Oh, I agree." He grinned and swept her hair back over her shoulder, stroking the back of his finger down her neck. "Your skin is so soft."

Tingling sensations were racing through her body at his touch. *God, I want you,* she thought. But as she'd said, the anticipation of making love with this man was electrifying. Her eyes dropped to his groin, his erection obvious in his denim jeans. She looked up at him from underneath her lashes. "I wonder how long we can hold out."

Nox grinned. "Personally speaking, and to be blunt, I think it would be amazing to be inside you right now ... But yes, let's keep this going until we don't have a choice. Why bow to society's pressure to rush into anything?"

Livia suddenly crushed her lips to his, sliding her hand over his groin and squeezing. God, he was *huge.* Nox gave a moan. "God, Livvy, try to make it easy on me, why don't you?"

She chuckled, loving that he'd used her nickname so soon. "Listen, you have all the cards here, Mr. Billionaire. This, at least, is on *my* terms."

Nox laughed, burying his face in her neck. "You smell so good, it's intoxicating."

She stroked his dark curls. "How is it I feel like I've known you forever?"

Nox sat up and studied her. She stroked the thick dark eyelashes she had been dreaming about, and he leaned into her touch. "I know, I feel that too."

She grinned at him. "Nox Renaud, we're going to have a lot of fun together."

And she meant it. She wanted to erase the haunted look in his eyes forever, even if this thing between them was only fleeting. The thought caused an unexpected shock of pain—already she felt so comfortable with him, they were so in tune with each other. A small voice inside her whispered, *you don't know him yet*, but she pushed it away. For now, they would have fun, and that was enough.

THEY SPENT a blissful two hours on the riverboat, and then took a cab back to the French Quarter to an upscale burger joint that Livia suggested. Nox didn't seem the type to turn his nose up at everyday fare and she was right, he practically swooned over the juicy burger, which was smothered in sautéed mushrooms and melted cheese. Livia grinned at him.

"It's good, right?"

"Damn good." He took a swig from his bottle of beer and she grinned, picking a stray mushroom from his cheek.

"I like a man who enjoys his burgers."

Nox muffled a belch in his fist and apologized. Livia chuckled. "Excuse me," he said and she kissed his cheek. There was already such a change in him now from when they had met. He was relaxed and laidback, and even the sadness in his eyes was less apparent. She couldn't believe it was because of *her*.

"Tell me more about yourself, Nox." Her smile faded a little and she looked at him steadily. "I'm so sorry about your family."

There it was, the wariness in his eyes, and he looked away from her for a moment. "I'm sorry," she said. "I shouldn't have said anything."

"No, it's okay," he said. He wound his fingers through hers. "I can't pretend it didn't happen and I want to be honest with you from the start. Yeah, it was rough. That doesn't begin to cover it, but for now I'll just say … it took some getting over."

"Can you get over something like that?"

He shrugged. "I don't know."

Livia stroked the back of his hand with her finger. "I think society places too much pressure on someone to 'get over' things. Why? Why *should* we get over things? Can't we just acknowledge that the pain will always hurt like hell, no matter how much time has passed? We just go on, live our lives, pretending we're okay when we're not." She cupped his face in her hand, her eyes locked on his. "That night in the garden, you were so honest with me. I asked you if you were okay and you said you weren't. Let's always be that honest with each other, whatever happens, wherever this goes. Deal?"

Nox's eyes were intense on hers. "How old are you, Livia Chatelaine? Because you have the wisdom of someone much, much older. Yes, of *course*, deal." He leaned over and kissed her. "We have so much to learn about each other, and I can't wait. One question … I'll be forty in two years and you're what, twenty-three, twenty-four?"

"Twenty-seven."

"Does the age gap bother you?"

Livia shifted around and sat on his lap, not caring if the other diners were watching them. She hooked her arms around his neck and nuzzled his nose. "You just said I was much older," she whispered to him. "So ... *what* age gap?"

Nox slid his hand under her shirt and stroked her belly as she kissed him. The feel of his big fingers against her skin made her weak. "God, I want you." She gave a small moan.

Nox grinned wickedly. "Anticipation, remember?"

She wriggled against his groin, feeling his cock harden almost instantly, and he groaned.

"You are a very bad girl, Livia Chatelaine. The moment I'm inside you can't come—excuse the pun—soon enough."

She hopped off his lap and smirked. "Anticipation ..."

"Devil woman." And they both laughed.

AMBER SIGHED as she saw Odelle approaching her. It was late afternoon at the salon and Amber had just had a blissful massage. The last thing she wanted was for Odelle to ruin her buzz. The blonde woman smiled tentatively at her but it didn't reach her eyes. That wasn't anything new with Odelle

"Always good to see you, Odelle," Amber said smoothly, and indicated the tea tray in front of her. "Won't you join me?"

Odelle nodded. "Thank you." She sat and Amber poured her some herbal tea.

"Did you enjoy Nox's party this year?" Amber was being facetious—she knew Odelle hated public gatherings. Odelle, despite her beauty, didn't mingle well with people and Amber had always wondered why. Odelle's famed iciness aside, she rarely made the effort to get to know other people, almost as if she were protecting herself from something. Odelle, Amber, Nox, and Roan had known each other since they were teenagers, but still Amber felt as if she had never really known Odelle. All she knew was that Roan had pursued the blonde woman, and that Odelle had only ever opened up to Nox, who she regarded as an older brother.

She studied Odelle now. The other woman looked tired. "Is everything okay with you, Odelle?"

"Of course. Roan and I are thinking of getting engaged."

Amber tried not to spit out her tea. "Really?" She couldn't help the tone of cynicism that crept into her voice, but she regretted it when Odelle flushed red with annoyance.

"Is it so hard to believe?"

"No, of course not, I'm sorry. It's just Roan never mentioned it. Are you sure you want to be tied to, let's just say, to a man who …"

"Can't keep it in his trousers?" Odelle's smile was bitter. "You think I don't know about his other women, Amber? Of course, I do. Maybe not *all* of them, but I have my suspicions." She looked hard at Amber, who met her gaze steadily.

"Then why would you marry him? Why not set your sights on someone else? Nox, for example. You adore him, and he thinks very highly of you."

"You think of our group as a revolving door of bedhopping and casual hookups, Amber. Nox is my *family*. Roan may have his peccadillos but I assure you, it's me who he comes home to."

Suddenly Amber realized why Odelle had sought her out. She was warning her off. She wanted to marry Roan—*Roan,* of all people—and was making sure that his friends knew he belonged to her. Amber gave a sad smile. Poor deluded Odelle.

"I believe you." Amber casually sipped her tea and they sat in silence for a while. When Odelle left, Amber pulled out her cellphone. She listened to the buzz at the other end of the line and when he answered, she didn't let him speak. "Roan, just how long has Odelle known about you and me? When did she find out we were fucking?"

ROAN HUNG up the phone and rubbed his eyes. *Fuck.* He and Amber had been so careful, but now Odelle knew he'd broken her one rule. *Don't shit where you sleep.* "I don't care about random hookups," she'd told him the night he'd first mentioned marriage. "I do care about you fucking around in our social circle."

And he had been careless. *Shit.* Marrying Odelle would secure his future—her father was richer than even Nox—and besides, he liked fucking her. He liked seeing behind the icy façade.

Fuck it. Now he would have to lose all his other girls and make nice with Odelle. He should never have started up with Amber again—Amber, who had nothing to lose by admitting their affair. And that was the allure of the redhead—she simply didn't give a crap about anyone. Except Nox, of course. Roan couldn't help the jealousy he felt towards his friend sometimes; Nox was just so damned *good*, it was infuriating.

Roan sighed and grabbed his cellphone. He would forget the crap with the women in his life and just focus on getting his shot together for the meeting with Nox and Sandor. He wanted in on their company. He was ready to grow up and he needed to focus, because there was one glaring problem in Roan's otherwise perfect life.

He was stone-cold broke.

CHAPTER SIX

After eating, they had wandered the streets, enjoying the atmosphere. Later in the evening, they found themselves at The Spotted Cat, a jazz venue that was jumping with music and crammed with people. Livia and Nox found standing room by the bar and ordered drinks. Livia looked excited. "I keep meaning to come here but never found the time."

Nox grinned at her. "Out of interest, how do you manage? I mean, I know you have the scholarship, but working at the café can't pay for everything. Actually, scratch that, it's none of my business."

She laughed. "It's okay. I get by. I've always had to fight for the basics so it's become second nature. Sharing with Morry helps, and I don't need a lot. Thank God for the scholarship, though."

Nox smiled at her openness. She really didn't care about money, and that was refreshing. He could imagine her happy with just a book and a sandwich—this wasn't a woman who needed diamonds and pearls. Of all the things he could give her, what she seemed to want was his time. He swept his hand into her hair and pulled her lips to his. "You're gorgeous," he murmured against her lips, "and I adore you."

Livia chuckled. "You barely know me, but I'll take that. You're not so bad yourself, rich boy."

Her words were totally without reproach and he felt her mouth curve up in a smile as he kissed her. A band was just setting up and when they began to play, Nox slid his arms around Livia's waist and pulled her back against his chest. Livia leaned back into him, comfortable with the intimacy already.

The band was wild, fun, and Nox lost track of time in the sweltering heat, the drink, the heady feeling of this beautiful woman in his arms. More and more people were cramming into the space and his arms tightened around Livia. She turned her head to smile at him and something shifted in both of them as their eyes caught. He pressed his lips to hers and she turned in his arms, her own wrapping around him. They forgot about the club, the music, the other people.

He gazed down at her and mouthed the words "come home with me." Livia's smile grew wide and she nodded. *Enough anticipation ...*

TWENTY MINUTES later and they were in a cab back to his mansion. Nox couldn't stop kissing her, tasting her lips, sweet from the liquor, his fingers tangling in her glorious mane.

He hardly remembered how they got to his bedroom but then he was sliding her dress straps down her shoulders and taking one pink nipple into his mouth. He heard her soft moan as she pulled his t-shirt over his head and he tumbled her onto the bed. Livia giggled as he blew a raspberry on her belly then proceeded to tug the rest of her dress and her underwear off. Her fingers went to his zipper as he returned to kiss her mouth, and he felt a wave of pleasure as she freed his cock from his pants.

Livia stroked him until his cock was so hard it was painful, but he resisted the temptation to plunge into her and instead made his way down the bed until he could bury his face in her sex. His tongue lashed around her clit and she shuddered and trembled as she became even more aroused.

"Nox ..." she whispered as her sex became swollen and sensitive, then he was back, kissing her mouth again.

She looked up at him with huge brown eyes that were shining and sleepy with desire. "Do you have a ...?"

He grinned. "Of course, sweetheart." He reached over and opened the drawer in his nightstand and pulled out a condom. "Want to help me with it?"

She grinned and helped him roll it down over his cock. "Big boy." She chuckled and yelped as he tickled her, but as he hitched her legs around his waist, she suddenly looked nervous.

"Are you okay?" Nox was concerned, but she nodded.

"I'm so good, Nox. I just want to savor this moment ..."

He grinned and slowly, his grin growing at her impatience, slid into her. Livia moaned softly. "You feel so good," she whispered and smiled up at him as they began to find their rhythm.

Nox kissed her throat then found her lips again. Her body was so soft, her breasts pillowy, and he admired the way her body undulated beneath him as they made love. As the intensity grew, their gazes locked and Nox began to thrust harder, faster, deeper, until Livia's back arched up and she cried out his name as she came. The sound of it tipped Nox over into his own climax and he came hard, groaning her name.

They collapsed back on the bed, laughing, panting for air. "I guess we didn't hold out for so long," Livia laughed and rolled onto her side. Nox enjoyed the feel of her breasts pressed up against him and looped an arm around her.

"Listen, I wanted to do that for at least a week, so we held out just fine." He laughed as she rolled her eyes.

"Okay, I'll let you have that one." She pressed her lips to his. "God, Nox, that was incredible."

"And only the start." He smoothed a hand down her side. "You have the body of a goddess."

She giggled. "Thank you. Speaking of incredible bodies ..." She bit down on his nipple gently. "I've been dreaming about this one nonstop all week. I even wrote some piano porn about you."

Nox laughed loudly. "Piano porn? I think I'm flattered, even if I'm not too sure what you mean."

Livia grinned. "It doesn't matter, I was just being silly." She kissed his chest then rested her chin on it. "Nice digs you have here." She looked around the palatial bedroom for the first time, and Nox watched for her reaction. "Actually, really nice."

Nox watched her check out the navy-painted walls, the fireplace stacked with wood—his bedroom could have come out of a Tommy Hilfiger ad.

Livia sat up and nodded. "I like your room. Classy, elegant—just like you." She grinned and ran her hand through his dark, messy curls. "Usually elegant." She looked at him for a long moment, and he was surprised to see her color.

"What is it, Liv?"

She bit her lower lip, hesitant. "Can I tell you something?"

"Of course." He stroked his finger down her cheek. "Anything."

"I've never ...I'm mean, I'm not a virgin, but I never knew it could be like that. Sex, I mean. So exhilarating, so ... overwhelming."

Nox was silent for a moment. "Baby, are you telling me you've never ...?"

"Had an orgasm? Yup," she was blushing furiously now. "I've

never let myself go like that. I honestly couldn't have cared less whether I lived or died at that moment, I felt so utterly blissed out. My whole body was ... *God*, I can't even describe it."

Nox chuckled. "Then I'm honored your first was with me. I promise to do my best to see you come like that every time."

Livia smiled. "I know it sounds ridiculous, but it means a lot to me. And it doesn't hurt, Mr. Renaud, that you are *gorgeous*. Seriously, look at you—who wouldn't come?"

"Ha, ha," he brushed off her compliment, embarrassed. "Liv, you know how you said you wanted honesty? That goes for when we're in bed too. If I do anything you don't like, tell me."

"And the same to you."

"Deal."

She snuggled into his arms. "So, what do you want to do now?"

Nox kissed her. "I'm starving, actually. Want something to eat, and I'll give you a tour of the rest of the house?"

Livia stuck her tongue in her cheek. "As long as you promise to show me every single ballroom in the place, I mean I've only seen the *main* ballroom and ... oww ... *oww*! Stop, you maniac!"

Nox tickled her until she couldn't breathe from laughing, then they showered together and wandered down to his kitchen.

"This looks familiar." Livia grinned at him as she hopped up onto a seat at the breakfast bar. "Is this your main kitchen or do you have eleven smaller ones for each meal?"

"Funny girl," Nick leaned over to kiss her. "No, just the one. It's big enough to feed all seventeen ballrooms though."

Livia laughed. "Can I help?"

"Nope, let me feed you, woman. Grilled cheese?"

"Perfection."

They chatted easily while he cooked, Livia admiring the way the muscles on his back flexed as he moved. He really was glorious. She adored the way his shaggy black curls fell around his head, the way his green eyes crinkled at the edges. She still couldn't quite believe she was there, that they had just made love, and that it had been even better than she had dreamed. It seemed somehow surreal, and yet to be with Nox was so natural. Livia studied him with unashamed lust, and when he caught her eye, he pushed the pan to the back of the stove and came to her.

"How," he murmured, brushing his lips against hers, "am I supposed to concentrate on cooking while you look at me like that?" He stepped closer and pulled her legs around him.

She was wearing his dress shirt—way too big for her, obviously—and he began to unbutton it, letting the fabric fall apart. He drew the pad of his thumb from her lips, down to her throat, between her breasts and down to her navel, making her shiver with desire. "You're so beautiful, Livvy."

God, this man ... She pulled his lips back to hers then, as they kissed, freed his cock from his jeans. Nox, grinning, produced a condom from the back pocket. "Always be prepared."

She laughed and rolled it onto him before guiding him inside her, moaning as he filled her entirely. "God, Nox ..."

He thrust hard into her, supporting her with his strong arms as they fucked. Livia bit his chest, kissing his neck and throat, before Nox ground his mouth down on hers. "Livia ..."

His cock reamed into her cunt so hard she thought she might slip from her position, and a second later they tumbled to the floor. Livia straddled him as they took each other to the edge of ecstasy all over again. Nox's fingers gripped her hips, pressing into the soft flesh as she rocked above him, taking him as deep as she could.

Livia came once then Nox flipped her onto her back and began to ram his hips as hard as he could, his cock growing harder and thicker, his hands pinning hers to the cool tile floor. Livia urged him on, coming again and again as he neared his peak. Finally, with a long moan, he came, shuddering and trembling, gasping for air. "God, Livia ...can we just do that all the time?"

"No complaints here." She grinned at him as he laughed, kissing her tenderly.

THE GRILLED cheese was unsalvageable so Nox made fresh sandwiches and they both ate as if they were starving. "It's all the energy we used up," Livia said, nodding her head wisely and making him laugh. "Don't mock. It's fact that sex uses up four-point-six megatons of kilojoule energy for every orgasm."

"You *just* made that up."

"All right I did, but still."

"Lunatic."

She stroked his face. "You're gorgeous."

He smirked. "Oh, I know." And he strutted around like a peacock, making her giggle.

"What was *that*? Mick Jagger crossed with a chicken?"

Nox gave up his comic strut. "Buzzkill."

Livia giggled. Gorgeous *and* funny. "Nox Renaud ... how on earth haven't you been snatched up by some woman already? I mean, apart from that face of yours, you're the full package, aren't you? I don't get why you would ever be single."

The smile cracked a little, faded, and Livia cursed herself. "Shit. I'm sorry. Did I put my foot in it again?"

Nox was silent for a moment, gathering his thoughts. He played with her fingers as he tried to decide what to say. "Liv ... when I was a teenager, there was someone. Ariel. We were inseparable, and we both knew it was inevitable that we would end up together. One night, I was getting ready to go pick her up for our senior prom. Amber—that's her twin sister—called the house in hysterics. Ariel was missing." A cloud passed over his handsome features and Livia took his hand, holding it tightly. He smiled at her gratefully before clearing his throat. "They found her body the next day, laid on one of the tombstones in the cemetery. She'd been st—" his voice broke and he looked away from her. Livia was horrified to see tears in his eyes. "Stabbed to death. And not quickly either. Whoever murdered her took his time."

"Oh, God, no." Livia felt cold. Poor, poor Ariel. The heartbreak on Nox's face was still obvious even though two decades had passed.

Nox looked at Livia now, his green eyes filled with pain. "I never thought anyone could ever ... not replace, I hate that word—and it's not true when you're talking about another human—but that I would meet someone who made my heart soar. I was wrong."

Livia touched his face. "I want to make you happy again, Nox Renaud."

He wrapped his arms around her. "You already have, Livia."

She kissed him, her heart pounding with sorrow for him. "What will your friends think about me? I mean, I know you're still friends with Amber ... will she think I'm just a gold-digging interloper?"

"No. Amber has always told me that she wants me to be happy. I think, for both of us, we had no closure over Ariel's death because whoever killed her is still out there. I think you and Amber would be good friends. I certainly hope so."

"On my part, I have no qualms ... except perhaps the total chasm in our social situations."

Nox shook his head. "You shouldn't fixate on that. Really."

"I promise," she smiled up at him, but then her face turned solemn. "I'm so sorry about Ariel. That's horrific. The police really had no clues?"

"None. Ariel was the sweetest person. No one could have had a reason to harm her."

Livia sighed. "Sadly, there doesn't seem to be much reason to kill a woman. Some do it just for the thrill."

Nox was silent for a while, but Livia felt his arms tighten around her. "When I heard you scream that night," he said softly, "when I saw it was you ..."

"That was just some dude trying to mug me, Nox. I dealt with it."

"Badass."

"You betcha."

He kissed the top of her head. "Okay, my little warrior woman. Let's go back to bed and keep each other up all night."

CHAPTER SEVEN

Livia's head was bent over her piano when she heard the commotion outside the practice room. She looked up as Charvi, followed by a couple of excited students, came into the room. Charvi looked stunned, overwhelmed, and shocked all at once. She nodded at Livia and then the piano.

"You might want to sit down and play that old wreck one last time."

Livia blinked, completely discombobulated. She had been working on her composition, *Night*—her 'piano porn,' as she had told Nox—and had been so into it that the sudden interruption made her shake her head. "What?"

Charvi smiled. "Your boyfriend is a *very* generous man." She turned as the wide doors of the music room were opened and a gang of workmen, huffing and puffing, wheeled in a vast trailer. Livia stood as they maneuvered the covered item onto the floor.

"You can take this one out," Charvi ordered them, tapping the piano Livia was working from, "save us the trouble."

The foreman shrugged. "Sure, no problem."

Livia quickly grabbed her stuff from the rather battered, but much-loved piano, even more confused. Charvi and her students grabbed the dust cloth on the new piano and pulled it off with a flourish. Livia couldn't help but gasp. Underneath the cloth sat the most beautiful instrument she'd ever seen. Charvi looked gleeful. "You know what this is?"

Livia nodded her head weakly. "It's a Steinway, a Model D Concert Grand Steinway." Her legs were shaking. Nox had done this? "It's Judy Carmichael's piano. Not hers personally, but her piano of choice."

Charvi was watching her. "That's right. And Nox donated not just one of these, but *four*. He's donated four of these babies to the university, plus countless other new instruments and a huge endowment."

Livia was shocked to her core and also conflicted. She and Nox had only been dating for two weeks ... and this was beyond generous.

One of the other students was looking at her enviously. "Damn, you must be good in bed."

"Tony." Charvi glared at the student. "That's enough."

"Sorry."

Livia shook her head. "It's okay. Four Steinways, though?"

Charvi looked at the other students. "Give us the room, will you?" After they had gone, Charvi sat Livia down on the new piano stool. "You look like you're about to collapse. Sit, breathe."

"I just ... I mean, what? What does this mean?"

Charvi nodded, but she didn't smile. "I think it means he's smitten."

"This is too much, Charvi. I mean, God ... it's been *two* weeks. Not that I'm not happy for the university, but ..." She opened the lid of the piano and began to press down on the keys. "God, listen to that tone ..." She began to play her composition, listening to the deep bass of Swedish steel and copper wire, the treble so sweet and pure. She played through all she had written so far—twice—forgetting Charvi was in the room.

Closing her eyes and moving her fingers over the smooth spruce keys, she lost herself in the composition. Livia thought not of the notes she had to play, but of Nox, and of making love with him, the fun and laughter they had shared over the last few days. They had become almost inseparable in such a short time …

She sighed and finished playing, opening her eyes. Charvi gave her a round of applause. "That, sister, is coming along nicely."

Livia grinned. "My piano porn?"

Charvi laughed. "I don't think we'll call it that in the program. Do you have another title?"

Livia flushed. "*Night.*"

Charvi sighed. "I guess it's no use now to ask you to be cautious with this man."

Livia felt stung. "Charvi …what is it? Why are you so nervous about my relationship with Nox Renaud?"

Charvi rubbed her eyes. "It's not Nox himself so much as it is the people who surround him. I worry about them affecting you."

Livia snorted. "Charvi, I can look after myself in that respect. Why is it I think you're keeping something from me? Tell me straight … is Nox dangerous? Tell me now before I fall in love with him, because that is a very real possibility."

Charvi looked upset, and as if she were about to say something, but then relented. "Just be cautious around his friends. If Nox is anything like Gabriella, then I wish you two nothing but happiness. She was the best person I ever knew."

"Then he is like his mother," Livia said softly, trying to keep the tone of reproach out of her voice and Charvi smiled apologetically.

"In that case …" Charvi patted her shoulder. "He might have donated the instruments, but you had already started to write that beautiful piece about him, and now you've given it his name. Have you invited him to the recital?"

"Not yet, but I will. I just have to make sure it's perfect."

"You will."

Livia looked at her watch. "I have to go thank him."

"Thank him for all of us, would you? Obviously, the dean will be writing to him to express his gratitude, but from me, from the music department and faculty, say thank you."

Livia hugged her teacher. "I will. And you know, I think he'd love to see you again."

Charvi's smile faded. "I'm not sure I'm ready. Gabriella was like a sister to me. Her death still hurts and I ..." She sighed. "I'm scared that if Nox has grown to look like his father too much, I might flip out on him and say all the terrible things I wanted to say to Tynan. So, not yet, please. Let me work my way up to it."

Livia nodded, sadness making her chest hurt. One moment in time and so many lives had been wrecked. "Of course. Let me just say ... Nox is a wonderful man. You won't find a more generous or kind and open man."

"I believe you. I just need time is all."

Roan stared at Nox, who looked back steadily. "After all that, just '*no?*'"

"Roan, you knew this was a long shot coming in here. If you need money, just ask, but we both know you're not cut out to be in this business."

"It's food importing!" Roan threw his hands up in the air and stood up. Nox could see he was agitated and shot a glance at a silent Sandor. Sandor cleared his throat.

"Roan, it's purely from a business standpoint. We've made our reputation on no drama and no gossip, by being above board and transparent on everything. And while you're a fantastic salesman, that's not who we are." He tried to lighten the mood. "It would be like Freddie Mercury joining ... Coldplay."

"Or the Allman brothers."

"Sigur Rós."

"Snoop Dogg joining the Spice Girls."

"You're Scary Spice."

"Am not."

Roan's mouth hitched up at one side as he tried not to smile. "Don't make me laugh. I'm mad at you guys."

"We're just saying we're too *staid* for you, buddy. Rather, this *company* is. Look, you want to talk about setting up a new company doing something entirely different, something that will suit you and that we could invest in, go for it."

Roan, mollified, sat back down. "You'd consider a new company?"

"Sure thing. Something where you'd be the lead and we would be silent partners."

Roan chewed on his lip, and Nox shot Sandor a meaningful look. Sandor nodded. "Look, I have to make some calls. How about I come back for you in twenty minutes and we'll grab some lunch?"

"Sure thing."

When they were alone, Nox looked at his friend. Roan seemed diminished somehow, stressed, not his usual ebullient self. "What is it, Roan? There's something going on with you, something more than wanting a new career."

Roan sighed and rubbed his face. "Don't worry about it."

"I *do* worry about it." Nox frowned. "Do you need money?"

Roan stayed silent. "You just have to ask," Nox said in a quiet, calm voice. Roan shook his head.

"Thank you, man, but I have to find my own way out of this."

"Surely Odelle's family ..." Nox trailed off as Roan laughed.

"Man, if I could keep it my pants maybe she wouldn't hate me right now."

"*Fuck,* Roan."

"That's what I do. Maybe I should start a male escort business."

Nox ignored that remark. "Odelle knows?"

"Yup."

"Who?"

Roan hesitated before looking at his friend. "Amber."

Nox rocked back. "You're kidding?"

"Nope."

"Jesus, Roan, don't you know not to sh—"

"Shit where you sleep? Yup. I'm that much of an idiot."

"Jeez."

Roan sighed. "Look, I'll work on Odelle, apologize, make it up to her. Marry her."

"Odelle may be a strange fish, but she won't fall for any fake sentiments or actions. If you marry her, you had better damn mean it. Or you'll have me to answer to, as well as Odie." Nox was irritated, but Roan held up his hands.

"I hear you." He studied his friend. "What about you? You made a move on the lovely Livia yet?"

Nox couldn't help his smile. "That is going very, very well, thanks. She's adorable."

"You bringing her to Thanksgiving? You can, you know. She can meet the gang."

Nox smiled, but didn't answer. "Look, get together an idea for the kind of business you'd like to run and we'll talk more, make a business plan. There's a couple of empty offices here you can use as a base. Don't harass the female staff, is all I ask."

"Would I?"

"*Yes.*"

Roan laughed. "I promise to be good. Thanks, man. I appreciate this."

"Just take it seriously. This could be a turning point."

Roan smiled at his friend. "You know, you're an excellent big brother."

Nox ignored the pain that shot through him—an excellent big brother, just like Teague had been—and hid it with a smile. "Damn straight. And I *will* kick your ass if you screw this up."

Roan stood and shook Nox's hand. "I swear to you, Nox, I won't let you down."

"Go tell that to Odelle."

"I will. Thanks, brother."

LIVIA WAITED as the receptionist tried not to stare at her. She smiled at the young woman, who flushed slightly. "Sorry."

Livia shrugged. "It's okay. What's your name?"

"Pia."

"Hey, Pia, I'm Liv. I'm kind of seeing your boss."

Pia smiled. She was young, early twenties, Livia guessed, with big blue eyes and jet-black hair. Gorgeous. "I know. He's such a great guy, great boss, too."

Livia smiled and wondered if Pia had a crush on her boss. She couldn't blame her. The next minute, Livia realized Nox *wasn't* the object of Pia's affection when Sandor came into the reception and handed her some notes. Pia flushed a deep scarlet and Livia hid a smile.

Sandor grinned at her. "Hey, Livvy, great to see you. Does Nox know you're here?"

She shook her head. "I told Pia I'd wait until he was free."

Sandor threw a smile at Pia, which made the young woman light up. "Nah, come on, it's only Roan who's in with him."

Sandor led her back to Nox's office. As she walked with him, she nudged his shoulder. "That girl has a king-sized crush on you."

Sandor rolled his eyes. "I'm old enough to be her father, Liv."

"So?"

Sandor laughed. "I'm not a cradle snatcher."

Livia felt a little sting—after all, there were twelve years between her and Nox. Sandor saw her smile falter and guessed what she was thinking. "*Totally* different situation," he said hurriedly. "I'm forty-five, Pia is *nineteen*."

"Ugh, okay, I get it. Don't tell Pia I told you."

Sandor knocked at Nox's door, grinning. "I won't. She's young, she'll find some young boy to fall in love with next week." He opened the door. "Hey, Renaud, found this little treasure in reception."

Nox looked delighted to see her. "Hey, beautiful, what a nice surprise." He came to greet her, kissing her on the mouth, lingering over it.

Roan snickered. "Get a room."

Livia, blushing, giggled. "Hey, Roan."

"I was just telling Nox here that we look forward to meeting you formally at Thanksgiving."

Livia rocked back a little. "*Formally?*"

Nox rolled his eyes. "He means *properly*, all of us. We'll talk about it over lunch. Guys, do you mind if I take a raincheck?"

"Nope."

"Not at all."

LIVIA TOOK him back to her apartment. He walked around the tiny kitchen/living space and nodded. "I like it. It suits you. Yeah, this is welcoming, warm. And even better, it smells like you—all soft flowers and fresh air."

Flushing, Livia was pleased. Her and Moriko's home was

small but they both loved it, decorating it with colored scarves and art pieces and books. The couch was big and squashy and Livia pushed Nox down on it before straddling him. "So, Mr. Renaud, before I feed you, there's a little matter of a huge 'thank you' to be discussed. Nox, I cannot believe your generosity. Thank you, on behalf of the university, the faculty, the students, and the music department. I'm overwhelmed."

"I thought you might appreciate practicing on the same instrument as your heroine," he said shyly, and Livia kissed him, crushing her lips against his.

"You're perfect," she whispered and sat up, unbuttoning her dress one button at a time, slowing peeling it off. She was naked underneath and Nox groaned, fixing his mouth on her nipple, sucking and teasing them both until they were unbearably sensitive. Livia opened his shirt and his fly, running her hands over his taut muscles, his flat belly. "God, I want you so badly."

With a growl, Nox tipped her to the floor, pressing her knees to her chest and taking her clit into his mouth. Livia gasped at the sensations he sent flooding through her.

"I'm supposed to be thanking *you*," she gasped and felt the vibration from his laugh rumble through her sex.

"You are," he said, his voice muffled. As he brought her to orgasm, she trembled and cried out his name. He moved up to kiss her mouth.

"When you call my name like that ... God, Livvy." He kissed her deeply, passionately. Livia pulled away from his kiss and made her way down his body, trailing her tongue down his chest, his belly, and then took his cock into her mouth, licking the salty pre-cum from the tip and running her tongue down the thick shaft. His fingers tangled in her hair as she worked on him, feeling his cock harden even more and quiver under her touch.

"Jesus, Livvy ..." She felt him jerk underneath her, and then his hands were under her shoulders, pulling her on top of him.

He slid a condom on and she spread her legs wide for him as he thrust into her. She moaned softly as they began to move together—really, there was nothing like the way he felt inside her, his cock so thick and long, harder than steel, yet the skin silky and soft.

They made love slowly, taking their time, their eyes never leaving the other's face. Livia had never felt a connection like this, had never experienced this intimacy so quickly with someone. She already knew the planes of his face, his mannerisms, the way his eyes would become more intense as they made love —as if she was the only thing he could see, or wanted to see. When they were this close, she wished she could sink into him, become one with him. Her fingernails dug into his firm, rounded buttocks now as he plunged into her again and again. *I could die right now and be happy,* she thought, and then pulled herself up. *Really? Oh shit.* She was falling in love with him.

No, no, no. It was too quick, too soon. *Calm down,* she told herself, burying her face in his neck and kissing his throat. *Just let it happen. Nox is the man for you and you know it ...*

"I'm crazy about you," he whispered suddenly and she nodded.

"And I, *you*, you gorgeous man." She kissed him, feeling a surge of certainty before all other thoughts were swept away and she was coming, riding her orgasm like a wave as Nox climaxed with her. She wondered if she should tell him she was already on birth control. Something in her wanted to feel his seed deep inside her, to feel his cock inside without any barrier. She was sensible though—they weren't yet at the stage where they could discuss that and she knew it. But God, to feel his skin against her ... would that be something he would go for? Her brain was too endorphin-soaked to think straight right then.

Nox's lips were against hers. "God, you're beautiful." He smoothed the hair away from her face. "Chocolate eyes."

She grinned. "Ocean eyes." He laughed and kissed her.

"So ... what were we talking about?"

"Your incredible generosity. Nox, you didn't need to do that."

Nox smiled good-naturedly. "I know, and it wasn't a 'thank you for screwing me' gift, so don't think that. It was time I did something for the university, and now I had a focus. Was Charvi pleased?"

Livia nodded. "She was."

"Good, I'm glad. I hope that we can meet soon."

Livia wriggled into his arms. "I did speak to her about that. Nox ... she's not ready. She told me she still has so much anger towards your father that if she saw you, saw that you looked like him, she might have some kind of left-brain-hip-check and freak out on you."

Nox was silent for a while. Livia studied him, her brow furrowed. "I hope I haven't upset you."

"No." But he sat up and rubbed his face. He picked his shirt up and started to put it on. "I guess, well ..."

"What?"

"I guess I should tell you. Charvi and my mom ... way before she was married to my dad, they were close. *Very* close."

"Lovers?"

Nox nodded. "I was the only one who knew. My mom used to confide in me and she always told me, although she never regretted marrying my dad and having Teague and me, that she hated being estranged from Charvi. That she had loved her entirely."

"Why did your mom leave her?"

Nox gave her a sad smile. "Family."

"Enough said. God, the tragedy of it all." She stroked his face. "Do you think that's why your father went crazy? He found out?"

"I don't know, Liv, I honestly don't. Dad was pretty open-minded, pretty progressive. I can't imagine he would freak out over something like that. Then again, I never imagined he could kill my mother and brother in cold blood."

Livia shivered. "My father was, or is, a drunk asshole, but he never laid a hand on me. I can't imagine what it must have been like for you."

He kissed her forehead. "That's the thing. He was a great dad. *Really* great. None of that machismo you-are-boys-so-you-must-be-tough and women-belong-in-the-kitchen crap. I guess I'll never understand."

Livia was quiet for a while. "Why did the police believe he was guilty so easily, then? Why didn't they look into it further?"

He looked surprised. "It was pretty cut and dried, sweetheart. They found Dad with the gun in his mouth, gunshot residue all over him."

"He could have been framed."

"Unlikely, according to the forensic team, but I appreciate you thinking well of him." He kissed her again. "What about you? You don't talk about your family that much."

She shrugged. "Not much to tell. Only child; Mom was amazing, but cancer doesn't discriminate. If the world was fair, it would have taken Dad."

"Do you think you'll ever see him again?"

"I doubt it. It's no loss, really. My family is here. Moriko and I met first semester in college and have been roommates ever since." She checked her watch. "Speaking of which, she's due home any minute so you might want to get dressed."

"Too late." The door was opening as Livia was speaking and a grinning Moriko strode in. "Hey, kids. *Nice* cock," she added admiringly to Nox, who was trying to cover himself with his jeans and laughing. Livia burst into giggles as she covered his groin with her body. Moriko's high laughter rang out as she disappeared into her room. "Let me know when you're somewhat decent and I'll come out."

A few minutes passed and Moriko stuck her head out of the door. She looked disappointed. "Oh. You're dressed. Give a girl a treat, why don't you?" She winked at Nox, who grinned back.

Livia shook her head. "You are terrible. Look, we're going to order pizza and beer—want in?"

"Hell, yes, if I'm not disturbing anything."

"Not at all."

When the pizza arrived, Livia passed out cold beers and they sat out on the tiny balcony that looked over the city. "If you squint," Moriko told Nox, "you can see Bourbon Street from here."

Nox looked in the direction of the famous street. "Really?"

"Squint harder ... harder ... now close your eyes and imagine Bourbon Street." Moriko cackled at her joke and Livia giggled, throwing a piece of pizza crust at her friend.

"Don't tease."

"No, no," Nox said, grinning, "that's what best friends are supposed to do to the paramour. It is the law."

Moriko nodded wisely. "You are wise, Young Padawan."

Livia coughed and it sounded suspiciously like 'geek.' Moriko smiled, cat-like. "You may mock, Liv, but me and *Wondercock* here are bonding."

Nox choked on his pizza, laughing, and Liv threw an apologetic look at him. "Sorry, she's not housetrained yet."

The three of them were having so much fun that Nox decided not to go back to work, and they spent the late afternoon and evening drinking and laughing. At ten p.m., Moriko got up. "Well, it's been swell, guys. I'm outtie."

"Hot date?"

"Tepid, but doable." Moriko threw her denim jacket on. She winked at Nox. "Good to meet you properly. Look after each other, kids." And she disappeared into the apartment. "And keep those windows open … it *reeks* of sex in here."

"Yeah, it *does*," mumbled a decidedly drunk Livia, with a satisfied grin. Nox laughed and hoisted her onto his lap.

"You're drunk."

"Yep." She kissed him. "And you're beautiful. Take me to bed, Renaud, and fuck the brains right out of me." She shrieked as he stood and threw her over his shoulder, carried her into her bedroom, and proceeded to do exactly as she asked.

If you want to continue reading this story, you can get your copy from your favorite vendor by searching for the title:

Secrets & Desires
A Christmas Romance (Season of Desire 1)

You can also find the e-book version by typing this link in your computer's browser:

https://www.hotandsteamyromance.com/products/secrets-desires-a-billionaire-romance-season-of-desire-1

OTHER BOOKS BY THIS AUTHOR

Saving Her Rescuer: A Billionaire & A Virgin Romance

I was just trying to get away from my crazy ex for the weekend when I ended up in a giant pileup on the highway up to Gore Mountain.

https://geni.us/SavingHerRescuer

∽

Sensual Sounds: A Rockstar Ménage

Lust. Lies. Double lives.

The rock and roll industry is full of people who are looking out for themselves and willing to do anything to rise to the top.

https://www.hotandsteamyromance.com/collections/frontpage/products/sensual-sounds-a-rockstar-menage

∽

On the Run: A Secret Baby Romance

Murder. Lies. Fraud. Just another day in the lives of billionaires and women on the run.

https://www.hotandsteamyromance.com/collections/frontpage/products/on-the-run-a-secret-baby-romance

∽

The Dirty Doctor's Touch: A Billionaire Doctor Romance

I am a master. An elitist. I am at the top of my field, and I know what I am doing.

https://www.hotandsteamyromance.com/collections/frontpage/products/the-dirty-doctor-s-touch-a-billionaire-doctor-romance

∼

The Hero She Needs: A Single Daddy Next Door Romance

He's the only man I've ever wanted…

https://www.hotandsteamyromance.com/collections/frontpage/products/the-hero-she-needs-a-single-daddy-next-door-romance

∼

You can find all of my books here

Hot and Steamy Romance

https://www.hotandsteamyromance.com

ABOUT THE AUTHOR

Mrs. Love writes about smart, sexy women and the hot alpha billionaires who love them. She has found her own happily ever after with her dream husband and adorable 6 and 2 year old kids.

Currently, Michelle is hard at work on the next book in the series, and trying to stay off the Internet.

"Thank you for supporting an indie author. Anything you can do, whether it be writing a review, or even simply telling a fellow reader that you enjoyed this. Thanks

Facebook

facebook.com/HotAndSteamyRomance

COPYRIGHT

©Copyright 2020 by Michelle Love - All rights Reserved
In no way is it legal to reproduce, duplicate, or transmit any part of this document in either electronic means or in printed format. Recording of this publication is strictly prohibited and any storage of this document is not allowed unless with written permission from the publisher. All rights are reserved. Respective authors own all copyrights not held by the publisher.

www.ingramcontent.com/pod-product-compliance
Lightning Source LLC
LaVergne TN
LVHW021719060526
838200LV00050B/2743